Marrying Friends

Mary Rechner

PROPELLER BOOKS

PORTLAND, OREGON • UNITED STATES OF AMERICA

First U.S. Edition, 2023

For further information, contact Propeller Books,
4325 NE Davis Street, Portland, Oregon 97213.

Cover and interior design by Dan DeWeese

Published by Propeller Books, Portland, Oregon.
ISBN 978-1-955593-06-9

10 9 8 7 6 5 4 3 2 1

www.propellerbooks.com

Marrying Friends

CONTENTS

The Playwright Sits Next to Her Sister

LISA'S SHOW had run two weeks as planned and tonight it was closing, neither a failure nor a success. The first decade of the new millennium was also drawing to a close, along with Lisa's thirties, her youth undeniably spent. The hand-washed air-dried wool sweater she wore kept her warm while she wrote plays, including the one about to begin.

Earlier, she'd rubbed on almond oil. What she detected now was not that.

Anxiété, an enduring scent.

The ornate theater was Off-Off-Broadway, originally for movies. The satin curtain and velvet-covered walls felt more boudoir than performance space, the balcony unstable, roped off. Some of the leather seats were ripped and some squeaked. The carpeting was worn and bunched; Lisa prayed no one would trip.

She usually waited until the house was dark before finding a seat in the back where she closed her eyes to imagine the actors finishing their make-up, finding their places, the stage manager here as in every show both schoolmarmish and earthy, deferent and superior during the last moments of bossing and ego-propping.

Tonight, because her sister Therese wanted "to be close to the action," they sat in the second row.

Lisa experienced her sister Therese as character-like in part due to costume: short skirt, silk blouse, red lipstick, décolletage, auburn curls both pinned and falling. Removing her fur jacket, Therese emitted bergamot, rosewood.

L'air du temps by Nina Ricci.

What would happen after the final curtain was predictable. She and Therese would have a couple drinks at a nearby bar, and then Therese would walk several blocks south to Penn Station to return to Long Island to her husband Mark, while Lisa would walk north to her fifth-floor apartment where she'd drink gin until she fell asleep.

Love and a big hit, her Great White Whales, continued to elude her.

As she waited for the house lights to dim, she feared the resentment rising from people's bodies. Some of them wished to be elsewhere: in bed sleeping, in a comfortable chair reading a book, eating something savory or sweet, drinking or smoking, seducing someone or being seduced.

Therese wasn't the only person in the theater wearing too much perfume.

Lisa was a SWF looking to meet a smart, kind, and steady man, but not online. Was it so horrible to talk to each other, or to sit quietly doing nothing for fifteen minutes? People were scrolling through their phones even if they'd come with someone.

Pretend it's yoga, Lisa suggested silently, pretend you're on a mat and a young woman with a flat stomach is commanding you to breathe, to let go.

"Was the lead actress fun to work with or a bitch?" Therese alternately petted her fur and eyed her program. She often confused the role of playwright with that of director. "Did you want to sleep with the male lead? Did you?"

Lisa pretended not to hear.

As a child Therese was the quintessential little sister, relaxed enough to be bawdy and darling enough to get away with it. As an adult she did whatever the hell she wanted, her wit an enticing contrast to her decadent hips and boobs and piles of hair.

Therese was an éclair, a tiramisu. She knew how to make jokes, how to apply metallic eye pencil. She wanted to be a mother, was about to become a mother: next week she and Mark were traveling to Bulgaria to complete their adoption of a little boy.

And me, thought Lisa, forever comparing, I write plays and teach theater part-time. She tried to come across as thoughtful and wry. Her appearance was deliberately austere. On good days she was a winter-flowering tree, on bad days a patch of dry grass.

After grad school at Columbia she refused to move to Los Angeles to write for television, though that's what playwrights did. Not because she was afraid! She loved New York City. She had history with the Atlantic. She didn't like LA's walls and gates and cars, its neighborhoods without sidewalks, its endless sunshine obscured by smog.

"Fear of success" was a phrase she did not think applied. She feared lack of success. She feared she would never find a man who loved her; she'd thought this last one, Larry, had been the one. Her fears were growing intertwined.

Lisa knew Therese feared little aside from drowning, which she almost did one summer in a rip tide when they were children. Lisa had led Therese into the surf, let go of her hand, run away.

Lisa was trying to make something, do something, prove something. Therese was a mountain or the sun, admired for existing. Yet the sisters shared a trait, one they shared with Mark. If "Why Stop Now?" were a song, it could be their theme song.

Unless you knew what to look for, you wouldn't see the signs. Plus people were often distracted or misdirected by their appearance, though this would soon change for herself and Therese. She was thirty-nine, Therese thirty-eight. They could possibly "look good for their age," but that wasn't really the same as youthful beauty.

Mark would probably be granted another decade of distinguished handsomeness—probably two.

The house lights dimmed.

If Lisa was being honest with herself, she *had* wanted to sleep with the male lead.

"Are you shitting your pants?" asked Therese.

Lisa squeezed her sister's forearm to shut her up; Therese responded best to physical cues.

She had seen this production of her play *Ode to Escape* before, but never with Therese sitting beside her. Shoulder to shoulder. She wondered if Therese could hear her heart beating fast and loud. She wondered what was it about her *really* Larry didn't like?

If Therese did not like *Ode to Escape*, she would not attempt to hide it.

"God," she would say after it was over, "that really sucked."

Now she opened a tin of cinnamon mints. "Want one?"

Lisa shook her head no.

As a child Therese sucked Red Hots, Atomic Fireballs. Lisa told herself Therese wanted things to hurt, though she'd been the one who'd pinched, poked, and punched.

Lisa wanted people to believe her plays. She wanted their essence, for a charmed time, to become the characters on stage. When it happened, if it happened, she felt a little godlike.

Therese's cinnamon breath seemed so steady she could be sleeping.

People did that too; they ignored Lisa's dream in favor of their own.

The house went dark. The red velvet curtain began to part.

"Oh boy," said Therese, crossing and uncrossing her glossy bare legs. "Here we go."

The Loop Trail

JOANNA DROVE her mother's car to the wake. "Turn left here," said her mother, but Joanna remembered the way to O'Malley & Sauer. All the Catholics in Lawnhurst had their wakes there, even if they were no longer practicing.

Joanna's mother Clara was wearing a black wool coat and tan silk scarf; Joanna wore a nubby pink shawl. It had looked perfectly great in Los Angeles, homemade in the best casually sweet way. Here on Long Island it looked idiotic. She should have borrowed one of her mother's old coats.

After parking the car, she and her mother approached the funeral parlor, where a bunch of guys were standing on the low flat steps. Joanna thought she recognized some of the faces from her high school Facebook group.

As she got closer to the crowded steps, the wake began taking on the vibe of her ten-year high school reunion. She had gone with Therese, who had not been married to Mark at that point, and their other girlfriends, all of them still single, and had remained in a corner, drinking red wine, smoking cigarettes, and flirting with a clump of boys who had teased her in middle school. She broke away from this knot only when Billy Idol's "White Wedding" came on, grabbing Therese's hand and pulling her out to the dance floor, their ankles wobbling in heels, Therese yelling, "I don't care anymore!" They were both drunk.

Clara pushed her way through the guys on the steps without waiting for them to step aside. "Hi," said Joanna, following her mother, gaze flitting over noses and mouths, eyes and chins. Therese had fooled around with most of them. Dave, Steve, Mike, Tony, George, Vinnie. No one born circa 1970 had been named Everett or Chandler or Austin or Ellis or Beckett, at least not on Long Island. Her brother Jude had been called Judy until eleventh grade, when his muscles finally caught up with his height.

Joanna wondered how long she would have to spend inside at the wake before she could join the men on the steps. The clutch of anxiety she had felt in her stomach the minute she stepped onto the plane in Los Angeles had not loosened. One of the guys out here was sure to have a flask.

The double doors of the funeral home were thick with white paint. Two funeral directors walked around in their charcoal suits, chatting mildly with everyone. Though no one knew these men outside the context of the funeral home, they were immediately and uniformly treated as intimates.

Clara didn't need any help; she understood the intricacies of wake protocol. She tilted her head toward the front of the room where the casket was, where Therese was surrounded by the girls (now women) from high school. Joanna followed her mother to the front. She should already be standing closest to Therese. She and Therese had been friends with these women, yes, but they had been seriously peripheral.

As they approached Therese and the casket, Joanna attempted mental contact with Mark. Remember rolling joints on my kitchen table when my mother wasn't home? You were so jovial! Remember kissing once when we were all stoned and Therese was in the bathroom?

Joanna worried that wherever Mark was, he was lonely. That was what the wake seemed to be proving. Mark was stuck in a box at the front of the room where people only went for a moment, knelt down, struggled through or faked a prayer, and then walked away to find someone who could have an actual conversation.

"Excuse me, girls." Clara employed the prickly voice she had used regularly when Joanna and Jude were young. She retained it now, almost exclusively, for requests of assistance in understaffed department stores. There was a murmur of miffed surprise from the women as they grudgingly stepped aside.

"Joanna!"

Joanna opened her arms and Therese fell into them, warm and cushiony and fragrant. She still wore *L'air du temps.* The rose and carnation appealed to Joanna, too. She'd tried to wear it once, but the scent felt out of character, a too-romantic costume.

"I'm so sorry for your loss." Clara placed a hand on Therese's back.

"It's okay, Mrs. Rambert," said Therese. "It's okay."

"I know Mark is in heaven."

Joanna didn't know how her mother could make such an uncomplicated and opinionated statement about the afterlife.

Therese pulled herself out of Joanna's arms. "Thanks, Mrs. Rambert. I appreciate that." She looked and sounded worn out in the exact way she had looked and sounded when they were in high school and hung out in the city at night and then raced to Penn Station with the hopes of getting the 2:15 a.m. train back to Lawnhurst. They were finished with drinks, boys, and dance clubs, and wanted to go home. They usually just missed the train and sat in Penn Station eating stale popcorn, waiting for the 4:45. Therese fantasized audibly about the fluffy pillows on her bed while Joanna smoked. Penn Station wasn't cleaned up back in the eighties, the smell a microcosm of the city's dualities: urine, sugary donuts, cigars, buttery popcorn. People with no place to go slept on the floor. Cops wandered by occasionally. The girls felt safe there.

"How are you, Therese?" asked Joanna. In the face of death, everything sounded tepid and lame.

"Not good," answered Therese. "I feel strange."

Joanna felt it strange to see her promiscuous high school friend in this new role as widow. The girls around Therese were drifting away. Joanna knew that a couple of them had fooled around with Mark before he and Therese had gotten together. More than fooled around, but that was back when everyone was constantly attracted to everyone else.

At the opposite end of the room the priest talking to Mark's parents looked East Indian. Joanna remembered this from the tail-end of her church-going days. Fewer of the priests had come from Brooklyn. The wakes she'd been to before were for her father and grandfather. Her grandfather had died of lung cancer. Several of her uncles had spent most of the wake smoking, more weary than defiant, in the designated lounge.

The crowd at Mark's wake was surging. The guys on the steps had come inside, including a little pack of men from the financial district, where Mark had worked. You could tell by their suits, which actually fit. Joanna wondered which of them had lost their jobs, which were becoming extra rich as a result of the current financial crisis, which had contributed, in any way, to Mark's stroke. She wondered if any of them were still in contact with her brother Jude.

"I don't feel well." Therese was swaying.

"Are you going to faint?" Clara grabbed one of Therese's elbows, happy to be needed. Joanna grabbed the other.

"Maybe I'm hungry? I haven't eaten."

"Come on." Joanna pulled Therese past Mark's casket. "We need to go out for a little while," she murmured to one of the balding funeral directors. "Can you help us?"

"Pardon me?" The man's shoulders were huge, like he regularly lifted weights.

"The widow is starving," said Clara, hooking her thumb at Therese.

"Follow me," said the funeral director, turning to a door that he had to unlock.

So they did.

The funeral director drove past two diners—everyone on Long Island had their favorite—before settling on one ten minutes from Lawnhurst. The diners' exteriors, plate glass windows, chrome and neon, and the interiors, vinyl booths along the walls, round ten-tops in the center, mirrored walls, were all basically the same.

The haughty Greek owner waved them inside.

"Sit wherever you like."

Therese ordered a hamburger "with a very small pile of fries."

"Onion rings and a Coke," requested Clara.

"I'll have a tuna sandwich on rye with lettuce." Joanna finished reading the impressive list of cocktails at the back of the menu; diners in Los Angeles did not serve booze. "And a Tom Collins."

"In that case," said Clara, "change my Coke to a Seven and Seven."

The waiter, a dapper man permanently impatient from years of serving stoned kids with the munchies, looked at Therese.

"Red wine," she said. "Just whatever."

Joanna's mother pulled a piece of bread from the basket the waiter had deposited on the table, buttered it, and handed it to Therese.

"Eat that," she said. "And drink your water. And then the wine won't be overwhelming."

Therese nodded and did as she was told. Joanna wished there had been a way to leave her mother at the wake, but there had been zero opportunity to palm her off on Therese's or Mark's parents, her contemporaries. If her mother weren't here she could really talk to Therese. On Facebook there were several pictures of Mark and Therese with the dark-haired boy they had adopted three months ago from Bulgaria. Aleksandar. In these photos Mark and Therese looked like all new parents: large smiles could not hide underlying expressions of shock resulting from parenthood. The boy— he was almost four— looked confused.

Therese was chewing her bread with her eyes closed, one hand around her glass of wine, as if the glass were an anchor. In the harsh light of the diner Clara's red lipstick was garishly orange. Therese's hair, which looked like it had been professionally blown out, was mashed down completely on one side. Joanna tried not to catch her own image flashing in the mirrors that lined the walls. Maybe tonight she would burn the pink shawl in her father's old backyard Weber after her mother went to sleep.

Even though they all looked terrible, Joanna felt a tremendous empathy for everyone in the diner. This always happened to her when she came home. She was never homesick in California, but when she came back to New York, everyone seemed so unself-consciously alive with their big noses and leather jackets, their shellacked nails and grating voices. She was even half in love with the funeral director who, once he understood the situation, had walked them briskly to his car and began driving so quickly that none of them had latched their seat belts. His urgency, combined with their lack of restraint, felt sexy. So did the fact that right now he was waiting outside for them with the car. "Take your time," he had told them. "I'll be here."

Joanna sipped her drink; the last time she'd had a Tom Collins was at Therese's wedding a decade ago. At the beginning of the reception, she had repeatedly shared pictures of her husband Sam and kids, Teddy and Bee, but after several cocktails had found herself sitting too close to one of Mark's stockbroker friends, murmuring jokes, listening to his stories about growing up in Queens, enjoying the feeling of his leg pressed against hers under the table, clicking into a deliciously flirtatious groove until she remembered she was married and reluctantly excused herself to the bathroom.

"I ordered the wrong thing," said Therese when the waiter arrived with their food in dishes lined up on his arm. She shook her head at the hamburger.

"No," said Clara. "It's perfect. Eat it."

"I wasn't always kind to Mark." Therese picked up the bottle of ketchup and began pouring some onto her plate. Joanna was surprised at how red it was and how quickly it came out.

"You were both very stressed." Clara matter-of-factly dipped a giant onion ring into Therese's ketchup. "You were worried about the adoption."

"This was after the adoption. This was on the day he died." Therese lifted her hamburger and took a bite. She chewed and cried at the same time.

Clara lifted another onion ring and then set it back down on her plate. She took a long sip of her Seven and Seven, sighed, and looked at Joanna.

This is where my out-of-town skills come in? Joanna wanted to ask her mother. You get to do the food and I get to probe about the unkindness? Her shawl had slid from the booth onto the floor beneath the table; she left it there. The only good thing was that Therese was methodically eating her hamburger, alternating each bite with sips of water and wine.

"We're all imperfect," Joanna began. She couldn't help but think of the priest at the funeral home; he must get this all the time. "We've all done things we wished we hadn't done." As usual she felt irritated by, as well as protective of, her mother. She took a bite of sandwich and waited for her mother or Therese to say more, but they were busy dipping Therese's last few fries into the ketchup. The onion rings were growing limp on Clara's plate. "Do you have a picture of Aleksandar?"

Therese pulled a photo from her purse and Clara plucked it out of her hand.

"Remarkable, isn't it? He looks just like Mark."

Joanna looked at the photo. Like Mark, Aleksandar had dark hair, but there the resemblance ended. "He's gorgeous."

"Yes." Therese smiled sadly. "What a crazy thing to have to tell a child. I'm already exhausted by the explanation. You're adopted and you won't get to know your adopted father because he's dead."

"Don't worry about that," said Clara.

"Why not?" Joanna was sick of her mother's easy answers.

"That boy is going to tire you out much more than a story ever could. That's what children do. They kill you little by little." Clara wiped her hands on her napkin and finished her drink.

Therese looked startled.

Joanna didn't concur out loud, but in fact when she was away from her own needy children, she felt more alive.

"I'm going to use the restroom," said Clara. "Then I'll pay the check."

Joanna didn't protest; she had promised Sam she wouldn't spend any money. She waited until her mother walked through the swinging doors to the bathrooms.

"So how are you?"

"Your mom's the same," said Therese. "I'm glad she's gone for a minute so I can tell you about me being a total cunt."

"Don't say that."

"Don't tell me what to say or not to say, Joanna. Your husband isn't dead. You weren't the one sucking the electrician's cock in the bedroom while your husband was snorting coke in the basement."

Joanna pretended not to notice that she was shocked by Therese's choice of words.

"I thought things were better since you got Aleksandar— I thought Mark's stroke…."

"Don't be inane, Joanna!"

Motherhood had made Joanna self-protective, as if that could somehow protect her children. She knew the world was a brutal place, but she no longer wanted to explore, see, or hear the gritty details. Sam rolled his eyes at all the movies she refused to see: no enslavement, no Holocaust, no sick children, no kidnapping of children, and so on.

"I was spending a lot of time on the computer," continued Therese, "meeting people." She leaned closer and Joanna could smell her perfume. "I knew Mark was desperately lonely."

Joanna grabbed an extra napkin to offer Therese before realizing that Therese had no intention of crying. She wished they had better props, like cigarettes, a better set in a less health-conscious era, a public plaza where smoke rose into a cloudless sky. Or even that they were communicating via e-mail; there would be time to compose something wise. The confused pain on Therese's face made Joanna think of Jude. One late night in the kitchen when they were teenagers, drunk and drinking a glass of water before they went to bed, Jude wore a similar expression. Joanna stood next to him, watched their reflections in the window above the sink. He turned and kissed her; she kissed him back, slightly repulsed, but also gratified. Over the years she had incubated that moment, but nothing had grown from remembering. She wished for something healing to say to Therese, some words of comfort, but all she could think of was, "How can I help?"

"You can't help me, Joanna. No one can. I just had to tell someone."

"Sam and I had to declare bankruptcy. Our business is defunct."

"Oh shit," said Therese. "I'm sorry."

"Girls!" Clara waved at them from the counter where she was waiting in line to pay. She pointed at the bowl of butter mints near the cash register, then wrapped a few in a napkin and stashed them in her pocket.

"Let's go," said Therese. "I'm supposed to be at my husband's wake."

Joanna stood with Therese on the steps of the diner, breathing cold air while they waited for Clara to leave a tip on the table. The funeral director was leaning against his car, texting, and Joanna felt her crush evaporate. She put her arm around Therese. Therese put her head on Joanna's shoulder. For a moment Therese's head felt heavier than one woman's head should weigh, and then it felt normal.

The next day, the morning was overcast. Joanna went on a walk with her mother on a blacktop path around a pond.

Just a few years before, the pond had been filthy, but due to work made possible by a grant for habitat restoration, it now attracted swans along with geese, cormorants, and a variety of ducks.

The path was covered with a thin layer of frost. Joanna wanted to hold her mother's arm, but was afraid she would shake her off. Joanna had been a famously clingy child. She'd occasionally wondered if, when her mother died, it would be her turn to thrive. Now that she was thirty-eight, it was becoming clear that a) Clara wasn't holding her back in any significant way and b) wasn't going to die anytime soon. Her mother still exuded an intense vitality.

At the far end of the pond, two enormous swans were building a nest on a rise, dipping their heads and long necks beneath the water, emerging with rotting leaves dripping from their bills, and tossing the leaves onto a growing pile.

Clara maintained a quick pace. She was seventy, and rather than curling up on the couch and watching more television than was good for her, she still worked full time at a bank, had added mindful meditation to her Catholicism, and made a point to walk or bike every day. "Shall we cross the street and keep walking?"

When there was a break in the traffic, they ran across the street to another section of the park. Here, instead of a manicured pond, a stream swirled through sandy riverbeds. A mallard and her ducklings disappeared inside the tunnel that went under the street they had just crossed.

"What are you going to wear tonight? I have my gray dress. Do you think that's all right?" A coquettish undertone rippled beneath Clara's question.

"You're coming again tonight?" Joanna knew she was glowering.

"Why shouldn't I go? I've known Therese since she was a kid. She used to date your brother, remember? She called to tell me about Mark. She invited me to the wake. She didn't say you can come one night, but not the next." Clara stopped walking. "We're friends."

Oh, really? Joanna was tempted to say. How much do you really know about your pal Therese? And when is the last time you saw Jude? Joanna hadn't seen him since Therese and Mark's wedding. She could find every kid from her high school graduating class online, but her own brother was determined to remain hidden. It appeared that for some reason his survival entailed cutting her off.

"How do you think Therese is doing?" Joanna knew her question sounded fishy.

"How do I think Therese is doing?" repeated Clara. This path they were on was a loop that would bring them back to the stream where the mallards disappeared. "Therese will never be the same again, ever. Her husband just died."

Was her mother implying that Joanna couldn't understand because her husband was still alive? She was always trying to catch up to her mother while her mother was determined to remain, not just ahead, but far ahead. Her mother was trying to lose her.

It was this kind of confusing train of thought that had led Joanna to therapy. Her therapist seemed more intrigued by stories about Jude and about her father than about her mother, but there just wasn't that much to say about either of them, at least in the present tense. Jude refused to have a relationship with her after she moved to California with Sam. She wasn't sure why. Maybe he felt abandoned? Maybe he resented her for leaving, while he stayed behind?

By the time she was sixteen and he was seventeen their father was dead.

She tried to explain it to her therapist this way: her father and brother only existed in the past. Her mother was slippery— she existed in the past and in the present. She was the woman she'd been, and the woman she was right now. In both iterations she was always so irritatingly sure of herself. Joanna had the urge to rattle her.

"Therese told me the truth about her and Mark."

"What truth?" asked Clara.

"Therese was fucking someone else! Mark had a drug problem!" Joanna was sweating. She felt as enraged at her mother as she did at sixteen, when she believed all the sad facts of the world to be her mother's fault.

"Why are you always so shocked about everything?"

It was a good question. Joanna did not attempt a reply. "Have you noticed this place is deserted?" she asked instead.

"Are you afraid?" asked her mother.

"Of course I'm not afraid." Joanna scanned the woods for a big stick. There might be a man darting through the bushes. Whenever a place felt devoid of people or when it was dark, she habitually thought of a dangerous man. She felt protective of her mother, but irritated too; her mother was the one always getting them into these precarious situations. Clara acted fearless, which made Joanna feel as though the burden of her actual vulnerability— how easily Clara could be hurt— rested entirely on her own shoulders.

Up ahead was an old building where the bathrooms were located. There were also seesaws and swings and a thing to climb on made of interlocking metal pipes. Joanna remembered playing here with Jude when they were kids. This wasn't a new brightly colored safety-oriented playground with a rubberized surface to fall on. The slide was literally thirty feet high. There was a metal merry-go-round. These were never installed in the refurbished playgrounds where she took her own children in Los Angeles. It was strange how often she forgot she even had children when she was with her mother.

She had to pee, but since it wasn't summer the bathrooms were undoubtedly locked. If there was a man in the bushes he was now waiting for them to get to the most remote point in the loop trail so he could jump out from behind the building and attack them. A man could easily be hiding inside one of those painted concrete tunnels it had been so much fun to jump on and slide off with Jude.

"Do you miss Dad?" If her father had been with them, Joanna knew she wouldn't be afraid.

"Yes," said Clara. "No."

"You do or you don't?"

"Your father was a hard man to live with."

"Really? How?"

"Joanna." Clara stopped walking. "I felt very alone."

"What about me and Jude?"

"Don't be obtuse. Tell me if you don't want to hear it. You asked, but maybe you don't want to know."

"I want to know." Joanna wasn't sure this was true.

"There were times I was so frustrated, so lonely, I used to wonder whether it might be better." Her mother's voice was sad. In the distance hummed the faint sound of traffic. Joanna strained to hear the rustle of leaves that would indicate from which direction the deranged man would spring. Instead she heard two short hoots followed by one long one. The sound came closer. It was two sounds, coming from opposite directions. Even she could ID that sound. Owls, calling back and forth. Her mother's expression changed; her eyes opened wide with delight.

"Well, do you know this?" Joanna felt the urge to destroy

Clara's easy pleasure. What was wrong with her mother? Joanna remembered her father with reverence. Her mother could be so hateful. "Do you know that several times growing up Jude asked me to kiss him and I did?"

"No," said her mother. "I knew you were close, but I didn't know about that." Clara's response came too quickly, as if she had been waiting years to say it. The skin on her face looked delicate, as though made out of a soft, clothlike paper.

"You didn't know or you didn't want to know?"

Her mother continued to look out at the trees. The owls were still audible. Joanna could hear their wings as they settled onto branches.

"Go ahead and press me," said her mother. "Squeeze me like a grape. I said I didn't know and I didn't know! Did I want to know? Would you want to know something like that? Sometimes I tried not to pay too much attention to you two."

"That's a really great parenting strategy. I'll have to try it." Joanna knew she sounded viciously self-righteous.

Clara laughed and started walking again. "What would I have done if I knew? Tell you not to kiss each other? Your kids aren't teenagers yet. Wait and see how easy it is to tell them what not to do." She was walking so quickly it looked like she might walk right out into the road that separated the two parts of the park.

Joanna took her mother's elbow and forced her to wait for a break in traffic. She felt ashamed, relieved, still angry.

"I'm sorry I didn't help you," said Clara. "I'm sorry if you've been troubled. Hurt. I'm sorry."

Together they crossed the street.

"Do you know," said Clara, musing as they walked, "that I've come to believe that there are worse things in the world than inappropriate sex?"

Joanna didn't know if she was referring to Therese and Mark or herself and Jude or maybe even her father. She knew the word "inappropriate" was a kind of blanket parents pulled from the closet out of helplessness; she used it on her own children. Her mother had apologized, but it didn't feel like enough.

What do you want, Joanna? The voice asking this question didn't belong to her mother. Clara was marching along, criticized, brittle, actively silent.

They walked back past the swans still building their nest. It didn't matter where the voice came from. Joanna could answer it. She didn't want to berate her mother. She wanted her brother to be more than a memory. She wanted to see Jude.

That night, the second night of the wake, reunion and bafflement were morphing into grief. Joanna again followed as Clara walked purposefully toward the casket.

Several women from high school holding onto one another. Crying teenagers filled an entire row of seats. Joanna had no idea where they'd come from. Maybe they were kids from the neighborhood? A babysitter of Aleksandar and her friends? The East Indian priest sat facing a man whose head was clasped in his hands— it looked like it might be Kevin Maloney from high school.

Mark's parents, Adam and Miriam, and Therese's parents, Alice and Paul, stood near Mark's coffin, receiving condolences. Clara touched Alice's arm and embraced her.

"God bless you," said Clara. "I'm so sorry for your loss." Tears filled her eyes.

Mark's mother Miriam stepped back. She had been ill with cancer for years and did not want to be hugged. Her snowy hairdo involved teasing and spray. Light gleamed through it.

Clara put her arms around Mark's dad, Adam, a tall, ancient, furrowed Mark. His chin was on his chest, his eyes closed. He opened them, and the group of parents turned expectantly as one to look at Joanna. It seemed silly to repeat exactly what her mother had said, as if she were her mother's Mini-Me.

"I'm so sorry about Mark." They would accept whatever imperfect effort she made; here she was still primarily a daughter. The irritation she'd felt against Clara tilted into acute sadness. Her mother had already lost her mate. The still-alive fathers were so tall. They emanated manliness and fiscal wisdom. A part of them still seemed in control enough to be bored by life. They still seemed solid, something to push against. In contrast the mothers, who had done the pushing all those years bearing and raising children, seemed to be shrinking, their biological imperative past relevant.

Joanna felt as though the mass of people at the wake were pressing in, suffocating her. Or maybe she just wanted to walk around and find someone she could talk to. The funeral parlor was comprised of a copious number of small adjoining rooms. She had the sudden irrational feeling that if she wandered around long enough she could find just the right room where her father would be sitting alone, perusing the sports page. He would look up; he would be so happy to see her.

Except for Miriam, Joanna proceeded to the hugs. Each of the parents wore a different cologne.

"You're a good friend," said Therese's father, Paul. One of the lower rims of his eyes was red and wet; it hurt to look at. "Do you still like California more than New York? Are you still living that glamorous life in Los Angeles?"

"Really, Paul. It's not the time." Gigantic pearls dotted Therese's mother Alice's powdery lobes.

Joanna wanted to say LA sucks when you're broke. She

wanted to say the loss of Mark's life leaves an enormous blank space we'll never fill, or, the one I'm really sorry for is Therese; except maybe Therese isn't that sad, maybe in fact she's been set free. She also quashed the urge to tell them that Mark had been an extraordinary kisser.

"California is very beautiful." Miriam's once-dark hair was now completely white, but her accusatory tone was the same. Each line on her face appeared etched by anger, hurt, disappointment, or the pain of battling cancer. "Last fall we went to Big Sur."

Joanna imagined Miriam sitting in an old beatnik coffee house, wearing a velour tracksuit and clean white sneakers.

It was extremely disorienting to see Therese step into the room from a door located next to Mark's casket. The door had been wallpapered over; Therese looked like she was stepping out of the wall. She was pulling her son by the hand, and walked past the coffin as if it were only a piece of furniture.

"Mom, will you watch Aleksandar?"

"Of course," said Alice.

Aleksandar pushed his stiff black shoes into the carpet.

Adam opened his eyes again. "Give the boy to me." He held out his arms. Therese handed him over. Aleksandar settled against Adam's body.

The presence of a child seemed to soothe all the grandparents.

Alexandar popped his thumb into his mouth.

Therese took Joanna's hand and pulled. Joanna walked guiltily past Mark, through the door in the wall. She still hadn't paused, knelt down, prayed.

"Check out this room." Therese sat down on an old-fashioned settee. The room was wallpapered in endless lines of faded roses. It had no window. Next to the settee there was an end table, and on it a square box of tissues. "My own little room. I'm a widow now. A widow in a little room."

Therese sounded like she might be losing it.

"Is it dumb to ask how you're doing?"

"All I can report is that I've decided not to kill myself. Can you imagine? The poor kid gets ripped from his culture only to have his spoiled fucked-up American parents commit double suicide. What would happen to Aleksandar? You saw them all out there. Our parents are old now. They aren't going to last."

Joanna sat down next to Therese. The settee was as hard and uncomfortable as it looked. This is what the wake was for, to show them that now everything was going to be different. Death wasn't some static event. It was pushing them out of their previous places. The funeral directors pretended to comfort, but really they were field guides shepherding everyone through the disorienting transition.

"Don't look so panicky, Joanna." A tiny grin flitted across Therese's face. "I said I'm not going to commit suicide. I just want to ask if you and Sam will take Aleksandar if something happens to me later on, down the road. Something like cancer. Don't look at me like that. It happens. Look at Miriam. It's not like I'm not planning to overdose or stick my head in the oven. Can I name you in my will? I know you guys are in financial trouble right now, but I'm sure it will get better. You're smart and talented. Your kids are sweet. Your husband isn't crazy. You know my sister is too much of a mess—Lisa's not even here. We don't know where she is. And Mark is an only child."

"Of course Sam and I will take Aleksandar." Joanna imagined the small-boned boy riding a tricycle on the sidewalk in front of her house while her own muscular preteens looped figure eights on their bikes in the street. It was a horrible thought, but she had it: they would be able to afford to raise Aleksandar if, after the death of Miriam and Adam, he inherited all of that family's money.

"Thank you," said Therese. "I have to get back." She stood up. So did Joanna. They were like too-big dolls in a too-small house.

"You know," said Therese. "When we finally got Aleksandar and brought him home, Mark was so freaking happy. He was literally crying himself to sleep with happiness every night. I was the one who didn't really know if I could do it. I was pretty sure I couldn't be a good mother. I wasn't good at being a wife." Therese smiled wryly, and Joanna took her hand—every part of Therese was succulent. "I've told you everything else, so I'll tell you this now too. I heard Mark fall in the basement. I forced the man I was with to leave, though he begged to stay and help. When the paramedics arrived it wasn't any use; at some point they stopped trying to revive Mark, and piled him onto a stretcher. Something opened up in me. I swear my heart ruptured. The paramedics didn't want to leave me alone, but I told them I couldn't go with them; my son was napping. Aleksandar had been home the whole time Mark was in the basement and I was locked in our bedroom with a man. How fucked up were we as parents? When the ambulance drove away, I ran into Aleksandar's room. I was sure that I would be punished. My husband was dead and so was my son. Aleksandar was in his toddler bed. He wasn't dead, but he wasn't asleep, either. He had his thumb in his mouth, his fingers curled around the satin trim of the blanket. He was looking out the window at this big fat robin sitting on the branch of the tree outside his window. It was so close to the window I could see every mark on its breast. It looked like it was looking at Aleksandar." Therese removed her hand from Joanna's and flipped her hair over her shoulders in a gesture from high school as the scent of her perfume filled the room.

In addition to feeling homesick when she was in New York, Joanna also often felt claustrophobic. This tiny room wasn't helping. Right now she felt like a character in a Greek myth that couldn't find her way out of the underworld. She placed her hand on the doorknob.

"One more thing." Therese suddenly looked excited and alive, and Joanna knew that whatever she was about to say was about a man she wanted to fuck. "Jude sent me a text. He's going to be here tomorrow. He's coming to the funeral."

The morning of the funeral mass was damp. Inside the church the air felt cloudy, as if filled with old dust, old incense, old prayers not strong enough to break through the roof, slowly disintegrating in the rafters. Mark's casket had been placed near the altar. Once again it was open. A kneeler was in front of it, but no one was kneeling there. Everyone was keeping a safe distance in the pews. Adam was holding Aleksandar, who appeared to be asleep on his grandfather's shoulder. Therese was sequestered between her parents and Mark's.

Joanna recognized many people in the church from the wake. It felt a little like the morning after a wedding reception, the breakfast where people either pretended they hadn't been drunk on the dance floor the night before, or relished telling the story of their antics. Only this was much quieter, more reserved. People smiled sadly at one another. Joanna didn't think she saw Jude. She'd seen a recent photo of him at her mother's house and had been startled by how much older he had become. It made her wonder what he would see when he saw her. Lines in her face? Gray in her hair? It was hard to believe that they were the same lithe people who had kissed on schoolyard jungle gyms in the moonlight.

Clara led the way down the center aisle of the church, genuflected, and slid into a pew. Joanna did not follow her, instead walking until she was directly in front of the altar. She stood staring at Christ on his cross. Lenny Kravitz, Mick Jagger, and the lead singer from the Black Crowes (she never remembered his name) all reminded her of this full-lipped narrow-hipped mostly naked Jesus hanging in the church of her childhood. She had received first communion here, been confirmed, and gotten married, all in exactly this spot. Then she'd tired of the Catholic version of the famous story: the Son suffering for the sins of the world; God the father with the power to forgive; Mary, the mother, confined to her alcove, allowed neither God-like status nor sex; the Holy Spirit wafting in like something out of Ghostbusters, completing the familial triangle. And look around, she used to argue in her head, the world is still full of sin and suffering. She began to enter churches as any tourist might, admiring the statues, patronizing the faithful. Catholicism was a language she had willed herself to forget. Only now she was wondering if some of what she had learned, albeit flawed, might be useful.

She knelt in front of Mark's casket and forced herself to study his face. He wore an impassive expression, one he had never used in real life. Joanna folded her hands into a giant fist. Okay, she directed at Mark. We both know Therese. She's thrilling and fun. She's daring and crazy. That's what we love about her, right? Mark's lack of response felt purposeful, passive-aggressive, detached. His skin was the wrong color, as if he were made of the same creamy substance as the flowers near his head. Joanna continued to talk to him as if he could hear every word. You knew what you were getting into and you went into it anyway. She wanted to shove Mark's shoulder, wake him up, beg him to quit horsing around, to come out, come out, wherever he was. Jude wasn't dead, but wasn't the effect basically the same? No. In this case, with this death there was a body, inert but real. She didn't know why she couldn't remember her father's funeral; deep down she had always worried that her father hadn't wanted to live, that he didn't love her enough to stick around and protect her. Mark had such a beautiful mouth. She touched his cold neck. She wouldn't realize she was crying until later, when she noticed her stomach no longer hurt.

People had begun rustling in the pews. She lifted her head and looked behind her. Everyone in the church was standing; all she could see was the backs of everyone's heads. Priests and altar boys were entering the church, processing down the center aisle. Joanna stood and walked quickly down the side aisle to her mother's pew. Clara was that woman in every church, the one seeking strength. A man in a charcoal suit stood closer to her mother than a stranger would stand. His gaze met Joanna's. Jude. For a moment she was back in the moonlit playground. She began to step over kneelers and climb past people at the end of the pew, working her way down the narrow space, trying not to trip or step on a foot. She knew that Jude wouldn't offer his hand and that they wouldn't hug. He would smell like cigarettes, and she would stand next to him.

Hot Skates

MARK'S FUNERAL mass was ending. Jude gestured to his mother *I'll be back after a smoke* and shouldered past his sister to get out of the pew. Outside he lit a cigarette, walked past the hearse parked at the curb, and continued east on Milton Road, an endless series of banks, bagel stores, pet stores, pharmacies, liquor stores, pizzerias, gas stations, bars, and delis. Technically it was spring, but his suit wasn't warm enough. He should have stopped at his mother's house and grabbed one of his father's old coats.

After a mile his cell phone buzzed with texts from Joanna.

On our way to cemetery.

What happened to you?

Jude walked another mile. He was en route to a graveyard too, the one where their father was buried. A low cement wall surrounded the place. Rather than a gate, there was simply a space in the wall, a sandy driveway he followed until it ended at a small white house, the administrative office.

Just beyond the office, grave markers consisted of metal plaques sinking into the ground. Elsewhere there were headstones of marble or granite. Like outside, inside the cemetery there were rich, poor, and middle-class neighborhoods.

Mark was being transported to a ritzy north shore cemetery; Jude imagined the funeral cortege, cars with their lights on, led by a cop on a motorcycle. Mark had been a stockbroker. Jude's father had taught high school math. He liked formulas and tables at the back of the text. Anything too abstract or speculative and his dad would take off his glasses and begin rubbing his temples.

A flock of starlings fanned out on the patchy grass, pecking as they moved mechanically forward; Jude followed. The birds were together for protection, probably, but there was a kind of aggressive sociability too, as they hopped along, looking for food. What were they eating? Insects? Bits of dirt? He didn't know. Cars careened along Milton Road. The birds were breathing exhaust-filled air. Also his cigarette smoke. *Grow up.* It was something his father had often said, without giving further instructions.

When his cigarette was spent Jude flicked it away, warmed his hands in his pockets while he walked. Not everyone felt reflexively guilty about smoking and everything else. Take his girlfriend Nan—she'd declined, without explanation, his invitation to come with him today. He envisioned her on a smoke break beside the back door of the bakery she co-owned in Brooklyn, her jet-black hair, the white apron she wore over her white T-shirt and black-and-white checkered pants. More than once he'd picked a piece of tobacco from her lip before kissing her. All the bakers she hired were handsome twenty-somethings, forearms covered in tattoos.

Jude reached the marble obelisk, the cemetery's tallest monument. He knew his father was nearby, but paused to read. Though the engraved words on the monument's base had been made illegible by weather and time, nearby was a painted sign:

THE MARINERS BURYING GROUND
215 PERSONS, MOSTLY IRISH AND ENGLISH IMMIGRANTS, DROWNED WHEN THE AMERICAN SHIPS BRISTOL AND MEXICO WERE WRECKED IN THE WINTER STORMS OF 1836-37, OFF THE SOUTH SHORE OF LONG ISLAND 139 BODIES WERE RECOVERED. THEY ARE BURIED NEAR THIS OBELISK.

Jude occasionally wrote copy like this—he hoped far less stilted. A freelance copywriter, his appreciation for historical markers was a remnant of his never-completed PhD. Almost three million people on Long Island and how many ever thought about the Algonquins who called the island *Paumanok*, "The Island that Pays Tribute." It was the Dutch name that stuck: *Lange Eylant*. American Studies—what a joke.

His father's gravestone was glossy gray granite. ROBERT RAMBERT 1942-1985, his mother's adjacent stone awaiting the inevitable: CLARA RAMBERT 1943-.

Jude sat down on his father's stone.

"Remember Mark, Pop? He fucking died. A stroke at forty. That's the official story."

"How's Therese?" Jude imagined his father asking. He would have called Therese "an old-fashioned bombshell," he'd have said, "a woman like that can't help herself." Even before his death his father had been stuck in a time warp maintaining fifties' era beliefs: women should have their own occupations, rituals, odors, clothing, codes. His father would have called Nan a "hot ticket," his greatest compliment. All Nan's bakers fell for her, and she occasionally slept with one. Jude didn't have the right to object since he still had sex with Therese, as he had on and off since high school, when she was Joanna's best friend, and before and after she became Mark's wife.

Jude's cell phone rang; it was Kevin.

"Are you here then?" Kevin's accent was diluted: Long Island, by way of Queens, by way of Ireland, which he'd left when he was three. Kevin's mother had come over in the late 1960's and Kevin maintained her lilting pattern of speech, sounding truly Irish only on the way to drunk.

"Yeah," said Jude. "I just left the church."

"Meet me at the Yellow Toad?"

"Sure." Jude could not help feeling there was something miraculous about hearing Kevin's voice while looking across the road at Hot Skates. In eighth grade on Friday nights he, Mark, and Kevin had roller-skated round and round to the Police, the Go-Gos, the Human League, sometimes in a squat with one leg outstretched, sometimes racing, sometimes holding hands with a bunch of other guys for a whip, skating faster and faster until the guy on the end was let go of, sent careening into the crowd.

"Bye, Pop." Jude patted his father's stone. Leaving his father always felt amicable, but unsatisfying and incomplete, the exact words he would use to describe their interactions when they were both alive.

"I'll have a Corona." Kevin was ordering at the bar when Jude arrived at the Yellow Toad. Like the other bars Jude had frequented with Kevin and Mark throughout the years, the Yellow Toad had never closed for renovation, the lacquered tables and vinyl stools remaining constant through the decades. Smoking by law was now prohibited, but the odor remained. Liquor bottles shimmered in the bar-length mirror. Tables lined the opposing wall.

"Coffee," ordered Jude, rubbing his hands together in an effort to warm them. "Decaf," he clarified.

"I'll have to brew it." The bartender looked approximately the same age as his mother, but she was fortified—sharp silver earrings, breastplate necklace, jagged stone rings, whereas his mother was austere—pearls in earlobes, gold wedding band.

"So brew it," said Jude.

"We're going to step outside for a moment, love." Kevin winked. "Back in a sec."

"Sure." The bartender's smile was exclusively for Kevin.

In the alley between the bar and the gas station, Jude lit a cigarette while Kevin filled a pipe and handed it over.

"Still pissed off as ever," said Kevin.

Jude took a hit and returned the pipe to Kevin. He was used to people attributing various emotional states to him. Usually it was women who thought he was something or other.

"You weren't at Mark's mass." Jude surprised himself by sounding accusatory. The guilt he'd felt, seeing Therese in the front pew of the church holding her little boy, again flooded his body. And then there was the look on his sister's face, her naked hopefulness.

"I couldn't make it." Kevin spoke without breathing, the way people do when getting high, palms up near his shoulders. "Had to work. Everything's always a fucking emergency." He exhaled. "Only now could I get away." He took another hit. "I noticed you didn't drag your ass to the wake last night."

Jude shrugged.

"I saw your sister there," said Kevin.

"I saw her this morning in the church," said Jude. "Was Sam with her last night?"

"Didn't you talk to her?" Kevin shook his head. "Sam's in LA with the kids."

"I can't believe Mark's dead," said Jude.

Not true. Mark's death felt lodged in Jude's chest like oozing tar.

"Therese is obviously devastated," said Kevin.

"Yeah." Another lie; Jude pushed the tip of his foot into a puddle where the asphalt was cracked. Of course on one level Therese must be bereft. But Therese did not live on one level. In the church she had maintained lingering eye contact, the telltale sign. She wanted him to call her. In the past he knew what a phone call would lead to, what he wanted it to lead to, but now he wasn't sure.

"You've still got Nan?" asked Kevin.

It always surprised Jude just how quickly his pleasure at seeing Kevin turned into distaste. Kevin's plumbers' coveralls were stained with grease; his hair was too long. He always pushed too close too fast. He brought shit up; he went where he wasn't invited; he didn't let shit go. Jude had always thought of Mark as the glue for the three of them, but perhaps he'd been more of a buffer.

"Nan's good," said Jude.

"Nan's hot," said Kevin. "She's like, twenty-seven?"

"Thirty-three," said Jude. "What about you? Anything serious?"

Kevin's laugh had a wheeze in it. "No more serious, not after the Michele debacle."

Jude thought of his father, who'd believed women were either as nourishing as bread or deliciously damaging, though the woman he knew best, his wife, was neither.

"Let's go back inside," said Jude. "I'm freezing my ass off. But first, one more." He held out his hand for the pipe.

Inside the bar the air was warm, enveloping. The beer for Kevin sat waiting for him, a lime jammed into the top of the bottle.

"Decaf?" Jude prodded the bartender as he and Kevin settled on stools.

"It's gonna be another minute." The bartender wore her hair in a style they used to call feathered. The door to the bar opened and shut. When the brightness faded, a girl was visible. "Hi there," said the bartender, reaching for a bottle of rum on the shelf behind her.

Except the girl wasn't a girl, but a thin, fine-boned, sinewy young woman. On the barstool next to Kevin she took a sip of the rum and coke the bartender placed in front of her.

"Hi hon," said Kevin.

"Hi to you," she said. "Hon."

Her windbreaker reminded Jude of a child's jacket, a red nylon shell lined with white cotton.

"I'm Kevin. My friend here is Jude. And you are?"

The woman looked at the bartender.

"They might be all right." The bartender laughed, years of smoke in her lungs. "And they might not."

"I'm all right," assured Kevin. "You can decide for yourself about Jude."

"What's with the suit, Jude?" asked the woman, not waiting for an answer. "It looks good on you." She ran a hand across her bangs, which parted for a moment before falling silkily back together. "I'm Kathleen."

Jude rode the six miles to Long Beach with Kevin and Kathleen in Kevin's van, still stoned, ignoring Joanna's texts.

You ditched us?

Jesus Christ!

Mom's upset!

Kathleen sat in the bucket seat next to Kevin. Jude sat cross-legged in the cavernous back, next to the plumbing equipment: wrenches, crowbar, snakes, metal tool boxes, rubber plungers. He indulged in imagined copy. *Long Beach, a barrier island less than a mile wide and three miles long, is home to 35,000 people and is known as the City by the Sea.*

Kevin turned on the radio and Jude spaced out further, remembering himself and Kevin and Mark in high school, in Mark's old Mercedes, going to Mark's house after school, and if Miriam was out, foraging beer, stealing and replacing Adam's *Playboys*, getting stoned, watching MTV.

"How long have you lived in Long Beach?" Kathleen was asking Kevin.

"About fifteen years."

"Long Beach is fancy now. The plumbing business must be good."

"The money's good. Hey!" Kevin's tone grew intentionally playful. "Jude and I are getting stoned today. Care to join us?"

"Okay." Kathleen sounded indifferent.

"Jude," said Kevin, "do the honors?" He reached back with the pot, lighter, and shiny black pipe.

Jude had had a pipe just like it. So did Mark. They'd bought them together eons ago in an East Village head shop; Jude had lost his almost immediately.

He packed Kevin's pipe, and passed it, along with a lighter, up to Kathleen. For a while the head shop where they'd bought the pipes had become a cell phone store. Now it was a restaurant for gourmet ramen noodles.

When they arrived in Long Beach, instead of walking up the ramp that led from the street to the boardwalk, Kevin led them beneath the boardwalk to get directly to the beach. They walked single file. Slants of light hit the dark sand. Jude wondered if Kathleen feared being between two men she didn't know. They were out in the open in the sun before he could suggest to Kevin they pause to take a couple more hits. He followed Kevin and Kathleen down to the ocean, at first across dry white sand and then, less awkwardly, on firm brown sand. His dress shoes had no traction. Hopping from foot to foot he pulled off the shoes and his socks, put his feet in the freezing water, a mistake. The beach was windy, deserted. In the bar the decaf had warmed him, but the warmth had been temporary.

When Jude was a kid his parents would drive to Long Beach on sunny winter Sundays after church. Back then the buildings lining the boardwalk were former hotels turned housing for welfare recipients, the elderly, the mentally ill. On the benches huddled people in dark clothing, like the photographs Jude had seen of immigrants on Ellis Island. Those hotels had been torn down, replaced with condominiums, like the one where Kevin lived.

Kevin was jumping onto one of the rock jetties that jutted out into the ocean, placed there at regular intervals in an attempt to thwart erosion. *Barrier islands constantly migrate toward the land; the whole system rolls over like a conveyer belt.* Jude knew a plaque at the beach would only get swept out to sea.

Jude watched as Kevin held out his hand and Kathleen took it, growing anxious as the two of them walked out further on the jetty. In summer there would be lifeguards blowing their whistles and running over to chase them off. Kevin had one arm curled around Kathleen's neck. He was tilting her chin. Kissing her.

"Are you crazy?" Jude yelled. He knew they couldn't hear him. He couldn't help feeling exhilarated. His pants were soaked to the knee. For months the winter sky had been gray, the low clouds *a mass of frozen crystals.* Today the sun was weak but finally visible. He had the urge to jump into the frothy waves.

Kevin and Kathleen stepped away from each other, Kevin laughing, thinning hair sticking up in the wind. Kathleen was looking back at Jude. There was something unnerving about her blank willingness. Kevin made his way back along the jetty toward the beach, jumping down to the sand.

"Let's go to my place," he yelled as he ran past Jude to keep ahead of the incoming tide. The shoreline was free of summer's jellyfish, horseshoe crabs, and shark egg cases. There were only broken shells and endless bits of plastic.

For a moment Kathleen stood on the jetty alone, facing the ocean, the hood of her windbreaker covering her hair. Was she hoping he and Kevin would disappear? Or waiting for a gigantic wave? Jude had little death fantasies all the time; he didn't know if other people did too. Kathleen turned around, hands in her pockets, and walked back down the jetty toward the beach.

In the mirrored elevator of Kevin's condo, Jude watched Kathleen's face, first wary, then bored, while Kevin described his new HD TV and the TiVo'd game they could watch. The construction of Kevin's building felt cheap, but Jude often wondered whether new things were cheaply made, or just new. Grow up.

"I don't usually follow sports," said Kathleen.

"What do you do follow?" asked Kevin.

"I don't follow anything. I work. I waitress Monday, Wednesday, and Friday. And I go to school." Kathleen smoothed her bangs. Her cuticles looked gnawed. "On Tuesdays and Thursdays I have class."

"And the weekends?"

"Life is different on the weekends."

"Isn't it then?" Kevin led them out of the elevator and unlocked the door. "This working stiff needs a shower." He took off his work boots near the door, emptied his pockets onto the coffee table, and used the remote to turn on the television, find the recorded game. "Knicks win this one." He grinned. "Jude. Take care of the lady. Find her something to drink." He walked down the carpeted hall to the bathroom.

Jude left his shoes on though his socks were damp. Kathleen kicked off her sneakers and sat down on the couch in the living room while Jude went to the kitchen and opened the refrigerator. Joanna was still sending messages.

You missed it.

Mark's coffin is in the ground.

"Beer or tequila?" called Jude. In addition to the booze, Kevin's refrigerator contained a half-gallon of 2% milk. Eggs. Butter. Mustard. Mayo. Oranges in a ripped-open red net. Neat leftovers in glass containers.

"Water, please." Kathleen sounded farther than one room away.

Jude felt a surge of lust, followed immediately by a memory of his mother.

Several months after his father died, his mother was sitting at the kitchen table, a glass of whiskey on a coaster in front of her.

"Your father could be a real sweetheart, but he was emotionally crippled," she'd said, answering a question Jude knew he hadn't asked. He'd been eighteen years old. Usually he remembered not to be alone with his mother.

In Kevin's living room, Kathleen sat on the couch. She was

still wearing her windbreaker. Jude kept on his suit jacket too. And his tie, which he tightened. He gave Kathleen her glass of water, took a swallow of beer, and sat down in an armchair. He'd watched lots of sports with his father, toughness in men his dad's corollary to beauty in women. His father loved it when a guy got injured but kept playing.

"What do you do?" asked Kathleen. "Where do you live?"

"I have a job in the city."

"Cool," she said. "Do you come out to the Island a lot?" She unzipped and pulled apart the edges of her jacket, as if to showcase her breasts.

"No," said Jude. "I came out this morning to go to a funeral."

"That sucks," she said. "Kevin told me about your friend who died. I'm sorry." She drank the water. The tall narrow glass was delicate. It seemed out of place in Kevin's apartment, in Kathleen's childish hands. "Do you want to talk about him?"

"I wouldn't know what to say."

"I get that."

With a small amount of encouragement Jude would have enjoyed trying to conjure Mark's gestures, his eager expression in anticipation of anything potentially excellent, like mind-altering substances or a group of pretty girls from another school in a house without parents. Jude could see Mark rubbing his hands together, lifting his eyebrows, basically licking his chops.

Jude searched his mind for something he could tell her about Mark that described a grown man.

"So how long have you and Kevin been friends?" Kathleen's white T-shirt was tight, her lips a cupid's bow, her hair glossy. A dead man couldn't hold her interest.

"We met when we were kids."

"You don't seem like you'd be friends."

"We were kids a long time ago."

Kathleen rubbed her forefinger around the rim of her glass. "Do you want to know if I have plans tonight?"

"Do I? Yes. I want to know if you have plans tonight." She was attractive, but her neediness reminded him of his sister.

"You mean other than this?" She smiled thinly as she looked at the pale yellow couch, the framed poster of the Islanders Dynasty 1980-1983, the plate glass window that could never be opened. She shrugged the jacket from her shoulders, swallowed the last of her water, and put the empty glass onto the table. Her knees had been together. Now they fell apart. "You saw me first."

"In the Yellow Toad," said Jude. He knew he sounded sour.

"What are you trying to say?"

"I saw you first in a bar called the *Yellow Toad*." He knew he would feel guilty later about being a dick, sad that the part of him that wanted to be kind had once again lost out. "I think Kevin saw you first."

Kathleen's eyes glittered with new energy. It was as if his disparagement was what she'd been craving.

"Why didn't you suggest we go into the city?" asked Kathleen. "Not that I could have. I have to be back home early tomorrow. I can't mess around with trains."

"I thought you didn't work on the weekends."

"I have my daughter on the weekends."

"You have a kid?"

"A kid, not a disease." Kathleen stood up. Her jacket remained on the couch, an unnecessary husk.

Jude leaned back and watched as she walked toward him. Her jeans were the low-rise variety. Since he had turned on the television, he'd been half watching the game, as well as half listening to the sound of Kevin's shower, Kevin singing in it.

A part of his brain had been daydreaming about the luxurious warmth of the water, feeling it on his own neck and across the broadest part of his back. The shower stopped. Kevin's song became louder, the words still obscured, though the tune was one Jude knew he knew.

"We could get out of here," he said, as Kathleen came closer. "There are places around here we could go."

"No." She was standing next to him, her knee against his knee. In another instant she was straddling his leg, the heat of her crotch pressing into his thigh. "I want to stay here." A faint sweetness remained on her breath from the rum. Jude could feel the warmth of her body rising beneath her T-shirt.

Mark had money, Kevin that charming accent, but women? They always wanted Jude.

"Irresistibly disinterested," Nan called him one night on the fire escape, flicking open her Zippo and sucking the cigarette to create a draw. "You're one lucky dog."

"Just need to get some clean clothes on." Kevin's voice traveled down the hallway. "Be there in a minute."

The pressure Kathleen exerted on Jude's thigh gained intensity.

At first he only entertained the urge to slide his hand beneath her t-shirt and bra, imagining the pleasure of his thumb across her nipple, and then he was doing it. It didn't matter how many breasts he had touched in exactly this same way. His dumb body always responded as if it was the first.

"Go on then." Kevin was leaning against the entry to the living room, where, in an older home, woodwork would be. Here the doorways were simply the ends of the walls.

Jude watched Kevin's flickering eyes take in the scene: beer bottle and glass on the coffee table, Kathleen's jacket on the couch, Kathleen on Jude's lap, one of Jude's hands at the small of her back.

Jude removed his other hand from beneath her satin bra.

"Shall I join you now or wait a bit?" Kevin's wet hair held the lines from his comb.

"Christ," said Jude.

"Now." Kathleen ground down onto Jude's thigh and pushed her forehead against his shoulder.

Kevin moved to stand behind Kathleen.

"Lift your arms," he said, and pulled off her T-shirt. "God yes," he said, kneeling down.

Jude's fingers met Kevin's at the thong emerging from Kathleen's jeans. He pulled his hand away. Kathleen began to unbutton his shirt.

"Do you know how much Mark knew about you and Therese?" murmured Kevin as he nuzzled Kathleen's neck. "Was he oblivious? I never worked up enough nerve to ask. Or do you think he knew, and found his wife sleeping with his best friend exciting? Was Mark the kind of man who enjoyed being hurt?"

"Who are you talking about?" Kathleen was petulant. "I'm here right now."

"Yes you are. Stand up, love, so I can help you." Kevin held Kathleen against himself with one hand, and unzipping her jeans with the other.

"I need to get going." Jude stood up. Kathleen's betrayed expression gave him momentary pause. He was objectively more attractive, higher status. The plumber was peeling her jeans.

Jude's phone began to buzz.

Why did you take off?

We should talk.

"Is that Nan?" Kevin's wolfish eyes gleamed. "Is she waiting for you in the city?"

Kathleen looked sullen. She turned her creamy body away, her bright white bra. Kevin lifted her in his arms. She wrapped her legs around him as if she was a child, and Kevin carried her down the hallway. Jude waited for her to look back over her shoulder, but she didn't.

After a moment of deliberation, he swiped Kevin's bag of pot and pipe from the coffee table, deposited them into the pocket of his suit, and rode the elevator down to the lobby. He'd walk on the beach, then head to a restaurant near the Long Island Rail Road, and wait for the sun to set before traveling back to the city. He liked the ride from Long Beach at night, a portion of the track snaking above the channel, lights glittering on black water.

After leaving Kevin's building, Jude stopped briefly in a parking lot to get high and turn off his phone.

Short Sale

FOR SAM, pornography was a toehold in a distilled, trouble-free world, the singular task ejaculation, the focused result sweet release.

The first time his wife had walked in on him at the computer since they'd moved to Riverside to live with his father, she'd turned around and walked out.

A week later Joanna walked in on him again.

"I'll be back in a minute," she said. "We have to talk."

Sam could hear her breathing on the other side of the door. He closed the laptop, zipped his pants.

Joanna reentered the room with the air of an impervious goddess. Hera, not Aphrodite. "What if one of the kids had walked in on you?"

"I knew they were watching television," said Sam.

Joanna knew when to let a statement hang. Their marriage was fifteen years old.

"This isn't about you," said Sam.

"Of course it isn't about me," said Joanna. She flopped backwards onto the bed.

Sam felt a simmering, adolescent rage, which Joanna either failed to detect or ignored.

In their early years, fights lasted hours or days, involved alcohol, screams, curses, slammed doors, thrown pots. They ended with sex. Pornography occasionally played a part in some of these brawls and sometimes starred.

For Joanna pornography had devolved from an airbrushed rival, to a stimulant they'd tried and failed to share, to tragic male privilege: consuming without seeming consequence, until it finally fell into the dustbin of sad habit. Porn.

Sam still felt hopeful when he looked at naked women.

"I'm trying to ignore it, but these brown tones are killing me." Joanna lifted and spread her arms to indict the room's beige walls, tan rug, and sand-colored bedspread.

During their marriage Sam had watched his wife change from art student to interior designer. Joanna equated happiness with well-decorated rooms.

"Don't blame me," said Sam. "My mother was a decent person who had terrible taste." They'd moved in after their business in Los Angeles failed. "And don't blame me for the economy, either. The rich people we worked for aren't rich anymore."

"The rich people are still rich." Joanna grabbed a pillow and slid it under her head.

She was right. Most of their former clients, thin, well-fed people, still flourished in Santa Monica, in Los Feliz, in Brentwood, in Studio City. Sam had observed many of them citing the poor economy as an excuse to pick up a pair of metaphorical clippers. They professed feeling badly about it, but he'd witnessed their deep satisfaction in the act of cutting back.

"This is the deal," said Joanna. The move into his father's house had made her chummy, chatty—she behaved as if they were college roomies. "Our lives," she continued. "The people we were. We have to let go of them. Those people aren't possible in Riverside."

For a decade in Los Angeles, clients had clamored for Sam's high-end finish carpentry and Joanna's idiosyncratic design. When the recession hit, clients stopped remodeling, cried poor. Worked dried up. Paying the mortgage became impossible.

It wasn't as simple as selling the house and moving to a less expensive area. Their Mar Vista neighborhood had not gentrified at the rate they'd anticipated.

The house they'd remodeled with soaring panes of glass plummeted in value. The amount they owed was far more than the house was worth.

"Why do some people thrive," moaned Joanna, pulling the pillow over her head, and speaking from this muffled cave, "while others get cast out? Did we have it coming to us? Did we tempt the fates?" On some level Joanna seemed to be enjoying their demise.

"Don't talk to me about fate. I not only live with my dad, I have to work for him. Today I spent eight hours unloading ornamental bushes so the people of the Inland Empire can plant ugly shrubs."

Joanna sat up, smoothed her hair. "What about that guy Enrique? Is it strange to work with an old friend from high school?"

"We were classmates, not friends. My father likes him more than he likes me."

"That's crazy," said Joanna, but Sam knew she knew it was true. Liking was too weak and limited a verb to describe what existed between family members. "Sam." She gestured toward the computer. "Seriously. It's been months. When are you going to make love to me?"

"I'm not myself," said Sam.

"Were you listening to me? You have to become someone else, someone new."

"I'm working on it," said Sam. "Maybe you can't tell. It's an internal process."

"Not necessarily." Joanna reached under the bed and pulled out five pound weights. "It can work from the outside in. Think of it like flipping a house."

"Only infinitely more difficult." The old Sam would never have projected such gloom. A house with good bones could be gutted, scraped clean. A giant Dumpster could be placed in the driveway, filled with offensive draperies, smelly rugs, stained wallpaper, worn linoleum, outdated appliances, and chandeliers whose fashionable moments had passed. And that was just the beginning. Walls could be broken with a sledgehammer, rooms painted and papered, floors lacquered, track lighting installed.

"Two sets of bicep curls," said Joanna, lifting purple plastic-coated weights, "and then let's go downstairs, kick the kids off the TV, and make dinner."

The next morning Sam and Joanna overslept their alarm, Sam's father left without him for the nursery, and Sam went along with Joanna to drop the kids off at school before she drove him to work.

The school was a utilitarian rectangle built in the eighties without any rococo touches of that decade. Sam watched as the kids disappeared through the doors, Bee first, her pink backpack shifting side to side as she ran, Teddy much later, his newly adolescent body having recently become part sloth.

When they'd first moved to Riverside, it had been hard for Sam to imagine the nondescript building containing a friend for Joanna. He had feared the move out of LA would make his wife sour and resentful, but instead she had taken on the role of plucky survivor. She "looked on the bright side," she "found the silver lining," she "saw the glass half full." Being the upbeat one in their relationship had been his job. As she rose to the occasion, he felt himself sinking.

When they arrived at the nursery, Joanna followed Sam inside to say good morning to his father and to apologize for oversleeping. The apology was both necessary and useless. Sam's father would neither forgive nor forget. Fortunately, he was nowhere to be seen; Sam knew the old man was in the bathroom. His medications made him need to pee frequently and loosened his bowels.

Enrique stood behind the cash register, conversing in Spanish with a woman buying a flat of portulacas.

Sam noted Joanna's interest in Enrique, her lingering gaze. Perhaps she was simply enjoying the beauty of the Spanish language, the profusion of pink and orange flowers. No, she was enjoying Enrique's thick black hair. How tall and lean he was. The three open buttons of his shirt. He exuded an aura of relaxed male completeness, which Sam remembered but no longer felt.

The customer left with her plants. Enrique paused, waiting for an introduction from Sam. When none came, he extended his hand.

"Pleased to meet you. I'm Enrique."

"Joanna," said Joanna. "The pleasure is all mine."

"My wife," said Sam, feeling stiff and stupid while Joanna and Enrique stood smiling at each other.

That evening after his shower Sam stood at the mirror to trim his beard. Each day he made sure to look into the mirror and thank the universe for his good fortune. He set his intention to work hard, to be kind, and to do no harm. Recently it had become necessary to put on his reading glasses to perform his daily ritual. His handsome face was aging, his skin beginning to sag.

Sam thought of Enrique's angular jaw. In high school Enrique had been a straight-laced track star, while Sam had been, if anything, a frequent user of mind-altering substances. Motivation had come later when he'd worked odd jobs in construction, and discovered his talent for working with wood.

Sam picked up his razor, shaving one cheek smooth and then the next, leaving a tuft of hair only on his chin. A soul patch.

"I am a completely confident man," he affirmed, leaning closer toward the mirror, the fog of his breath obscuring his face.

In the car on the way to work the next morning, his father cursing and screaming, ostensibly at other drivers, Sam felt his childhood flood back and try to drown him.

He believed his victories in life were the direct result of a disciplined effort to keep the past at bay, to stay focused not only on the present, but on the positive possibilities of the future. Every moment of every day was an opportunity to be constructive. Thus, while his father yelled and gesticulated, Sam made a mental inventory of the nursery's cramped, fluorescent-lit interior. He must find ways to improve his father's crappy, old-fashioned plant nursery.

The register was located near the front door, near racks of seed packets, bags of potting soil, and shelves filled with house plants, hand tools, and fertilizers. The store looked much as it had when Sam worked there in high school. Most of the garden tchotchkes (glass mushrooms, ceramic doves, wrought iron spikes topped with teacups and saucers) were unchanged. Only the large table devoted to the needs of garden fairies was new. Diminutive houses made from what looked like dripped wet sand. Tiny wrought iron benches, bridges, and swing sets. Minuscule fairy stepping-stones, glazed in a rainbow of colors. At first Sam had been surprised by his father's inclusion of this whimsy, but soon he saw the fairy stuff made serious money. Almost every customer lingered at the table, fondling the teensy items. Most customers bought something, and often bought many things, claiming their intent to enchant their children, grandchildren, or the kids next door.

"Goddammit! Stay in your own fucking lane!" Sam's father leaned long on the horn, and Sam reminded himself that the blare could not realistically have the same effect as the punches and slaps his father had given so freely in Sam's youth, until Sam's mother had threatened to leave.

Road workers appeared ahead. Sam's father slammed on the brakes. He remained hunched over the wheel, muttering. "Fix the roads at night, you fucking assholes."

As they sat waiting for permission to move forward, Sam cracked his window and turned towards it. He imagined his father's negativity glancing off his shoulder, floating out the window, and dissipating like a poisonous emission.

The road worker turned his STOP sign around to reveal SLOW and waved them forward. Sam's father flipped him the bird.

"How's it going?" said Enrique when Sam and his father arrived at the nursery.

"It's going fucking great," said Sam's father. It took several attempts for him to grab the silver tab of the zipper on his jacket. "Except it's already too damn hot."

"I made coffee." Enrique gestured toward the coffeemaker and went outside.

Sam straightened seed packets on the rack, and looked out the plate glass doors to the long tables holding shade-loving plants: impatiens, coleus, lobelia. They were healthy and vigorous due to the simple canopies Enrique had built with old lumber and black landscaping cloth.

When he was a teenager, Sam had attributed the nursery's success to his father's brutal work ethic, his savvy acumen. Now he understood the nursery remained in business solely due to Enrique's hard work. In the past, Sam had felt grateful to Enrique for tolerating the old man. Things had changed. His own prospects severely limited, Sam could no longer afford to be sanguine. Like it or not, Enrique had become a rival. Most of the nursery's steady customers were Spanish speaking. Enrique made sure all of the signs were bilingual. *Las Hadas*, read one such sign, and beneath it, *Fairies*. Sam watched as Enrique hauled bags of compost closer to the door.

Enrique lived in the same neighborhood as the nursery. He began work early every morning in order to be with his kids after school while his wife was at the hospital, where she worked as a nurse. From the high school grapevine Sam knew that back in the day a knee injury had forced Enrique to give up his athletic scholarship at Cal Poly Pomona; he knew Enrique's life had gone through a difficult stretch: addiction to painkillers.

"Leave those seeds alone." Sam's father bumped into Sam as he walked by. It was an ancient habit; his father never left enough room to get by. "Go out there and figure out how to sell all those goddamn dwarf pines."

Sam gulped the rest of his coffee. The life he and Joanna had inhabited in Los Angeles still existed, but their access had been terminated. There would be no more platters of icy shrimp, sugary poolside cocktails, or bohemian dinners with vintners and music video producers. In Los Angeles, through diligence and good luck, Sam had grown into the fulfilled husband and father he'd always wanted to be, but life had shoved him back to Riverside, where the desert sun was unrelenting. Sam felt a babyish longing for the ocean. He found himself griping at Enrique as he walked outside.

"I don't think that's the best spot for the compost. I'd leave the bags near the fence, so people don't have to haul them too far to their cars."

"That's what you'd do?" Enrique's voice was mild, but Sam saw the twitch in his jaw.

There wasn't enough work at the nursery for three men. There was barely enough for two, which was why things had worked so well for Enrique and the old man. Sam's father wandered around while Enrique was free to run the place, which had survived Home Depot and Lowe's and Walmart and Target. Enrique had reached out to his neighbors, people he had grown up with, people he treated well. He gave them good service and excellent value, and they rewarded him with their loyalty. In the early days, Latinos had come to the nursery as day laborers and employees of rich whites. Now they were owners of businesses and homes.

"Yeah, that's exactly what I would do," said Sam.

Enrique's nostrils flared, but he said nothing as he walked back toward the bags of compost.

Sam trailed behind him. "You have to think about the needs of the customer!" He knew he should leave Enrique alone, but he could not. For years he had successfully quelled his desire to pester, needle, or hurt other people, but now this resolve felt unnecessary. He was tired of being respectful. Where had it gotten him?

"Are you listening to me?" Sam reached out to grab

Enrique's elbow. Enrique jerked away and spun around to face Sam. Sam felt the asphalt lot become a rushing creek he had to call across in order to be heard. "What I try to do at every moment is to imagine the customer's experience!" He raised his hand to sagely stroke his beard, and felt only the stubbly patch of hair on his chin. He took a step closer to Enrique.

Enrique's eyes narrowed, and he took a step back.

Sam dropped his voice. "I ask myself, how does the customer move through time and space while in this dream we call the plant nursery?"

"For Christ's sake," hollered the old man. He was coming at Enrique too, holding out the notebook they used to track orders. "Dreaming won't pay the fucking bills." He thrust the notebook at Enrique, bumping against him as he moved past.

Disgust and forbearance competed on Enrique's face. It was the same combination of feelings Sam had been struggling with since returning to his father's house, his father's business. This recognition changed nothing; Sam still felt the urge to bait and berate.

"Are you going to move that compost away from the door and closer to the fence?" asked Sam. "Because if you won't, I will." He reached out to push Enrique's shoulder for emphasis, and saw too late: Enrique had had enough. He was yelling something unintelligible, rearing back, swinging at Sam, knuckles missing Sam's face and landing instead on his collarbone. Sam staggered backwards before crouching on the asphalt; tears burned his eyes. There was no satisfying breakage or blood; the men would only be mottled or swollen. When Sam opened his eyes, his father's cracked leather shoes were next to Enrique's work boots.

"I lost my temper." Enrique sounded deflated, dazed.

"Take lunch," said the old man. "When you get back, order

more annuals, and watch the fucking price! Those cocksuckers are always trying to dick us over."

Sam waited. In the cracks of the asphalt crowded pale weeds.

"You shouldn't have done that," said Sam's father when Enrique was gone. Sam watched his father's feet. If the old man kicked him, he would rise up, strangle him, and toss his body onto the pile of compost. But his father shuffled off, farting en route to the bathroom.

Sam stood. He looked around, surprised to find the nursery just as it had been before he'd been hit. For a moment he considered running around like one of the escaped chimps in the recent *Planet of the Apes* movie, hooting and smashing the tables, shade canopies, plants. His collarbone ached. A rush of bitter regret shot through his body. Yes he was white, but there had been so many men of all ages, of all races he'd worked with over the years and gotten along with well, so many carpenters, contractors, plumbers, electricians; he'd felt himself to be a member of a brotherhood that still got dirty every day, men who used their hands to make and fix things.

He found his water bottle inside on the fairy table. He took a long drink. They didn't sell actual fairies. Fairies weren't like Barbie dolls; you didn't buy the people first and then their clothes and houses and cars. No. You bought the fairy stuff to thereby entice the fairies into being. You had to believe the fairies—Sam imagined tiny nude curvaceous women waving magic wands—would come. Some of the stones were etched with evocative italicized words. He pushed one such rock into the pocket of his jeans, and went out to deal with the pines.

The A-Frame

THE SUN rose as Lisa drove into town to get water from the spring. It was April, but essentially still winter, temperatures at night dipped below freezing. Hard old snow glittered on roofs and lawns. All the houses and buildings in these northern Vermont towns were old, but genteel and picturesque. It wasn't easy to maintain this beauty. Lisa had never seen so many carpenters, stonemasons, and painters in her life.

As she drove, she visualized a dearth of people the way she had in the city when she walked to the public pool to swim laps. That visualization always proved futile. Empty lanes did not exist in New York's indoor public pools. Everyone swam inches from the people in front of and behind, fingers brushing toes.

At the spring a mason had cemented stones together to make a wall; the wall lent grandeur to what was essentially water coming out of a metal pipe. Three men were already there getting water. They looked approximately Lisa's age, one she was beginning, if it ever came up in conversation, to keep approximate.

Each of the men held a container. As far as waiting went, three people with one container each wasn't a big deal, but it had been over a month since she had spoken to anyone at length. If she didn't get in line, however, and waited in her truck for the men to go away, another person believing in the marvelous powers of spring water (or, like her, with no access to drinking water) could drive up with any number of empty containers and she'd have to wait.

Lisa lifted the first of the large water tanks out of the truck bed and brought it to where the men were standing.

"Hey," said the shortest of the trio. He wore a paint-splattered baseball cap. Now that she was closer, she could see that the men were quite young, probably in their late twenties.

"Hey," she responded, aware that her uncombed hair, old sneakers, holey jeans, knitted cardigan sweater, and fur-trimmed parka sent possibly intriguing signals. She could be a yoga instructor, flexible and willing. She could be a locavore, a jam maker and bread baker, the perfect complement for a hungry man. She could be vaguely creative and independently wealthy: her assessment of them.

The guy filling an empty jar had long blond hair. The guy wearing a puffy red vest drank the last of the milk from a plastic gallon. Lisa noted his vulnerable throat, and to secure her place in line, placed her water tank behind the man in the ball cap.

"Need a hand with the rest?" He gestured toward the truck.

"No thanks." She walked back to the truck, retrieved another tank, and placed it behind the first. The guy in the red vest looked hungry as well as thirsty, but perhaps he was just tall and thin.

"We're sculptors. A collective." The man in the cap finished filling what had been a carton of orange juice and stepped aside. "We're doing a residency at the arts center." He gestured across the street.

The man in the red vest scowled and began filling Lisa's water tank. Her eyes met his and she felt a jolt.

The man in the cap hooked his thumb toward the truck. "Let me help. My good deed for the day."

"The Dalai Lama asks for good deeds all day long." Lisa thought she'd forgotten how to flirt, but her parka was helpfully unzipped, and the blouse beneath her sweater only partially buttoned.

"Then I'd better start now," said the man in the cap.

The man in the red vest muttered something unintelligible and gave Lisa's water tank a slight kick. It was a childish, attention-getting gesture. He began filling her second tank. The blond man was sitting on a bench near the spring. He finished rolling a cigarette and lit a match. "I'm Karl. That's Sean." He used his cigarette to point to the man in the red vest.

"I'm Mateo," said the man in the ball cap, returning to the spring with the last of Lisa's containers.

"*Matthew* is from New Jersey," said Karl. "He went to Santa Fe a few months ago and came back with a new name."

"I grew up on Long Island," said Lisa, attempting solidarity.

"Well," Karl exhaled dramatically. "We must be off."

"You asshole." Mateo flipped his cap backwards and turned toward Lisa "I didn't catch your name."

"Lisa."

"Lisa from Long Island. Listen." Karl stashed the tobacco in his pocket. At some level he must at all times be aware of his glorious hair. "Tonight is what we call Open Studios at the center. Wine, cheese, small talk. Eight o'clock. Come look at our etchings."

Lisa had spent the months of January and February at the center, which consisted of several small white houses surrounding a larger central white house.

Her friend Joy was still there. Joy had been granted a yearlong residency in recognition and encouragement of her exceptional promise in two art forms; Joy painted and wrote poetry.

Lisa had also worked on two projects during her time at the center: writing a new play and not drinking.

"Please," said Mateo. "Join us. Save us from the artists and writers." He removed and resettled his cap. "Be a real person."

Lisa saw Sean looking at her through his long eyelashes.

"I can't." She pulled one tank away from the mouth of the pipe and slid another in its place. "I write plays."

Mateo grinned. "Come anyway."

Karl and Sean crossed the street back to the arts center. Mateo ran to catch up. Sean looked over his shoulder and stared; Lisa stared back until he turned around. She tried not to be annoyed that they hadn't stuck around long enough to help her slide the water-filled tanks up her makeshift ramp into the back of the truck.

That afternoon Lisa was back at the A-Frame in the woods she began renting in March after failing to finish writing her play at the arts center during her residency in January and February. In the A-Frame she stopped reading email or checking her P.O. box. When her cell phone died, she did not recharge it.

She was trying to finish her project, though she was experienced enough to know that to successfully develop a new play, she needed to workshop it with actors. But she didn't want to return to New York without a new play in hand, or while she was still a drunk.

Her play was set on a Long Island beach in the summer. It featured three characters, a husband and wife arguing furiously about something they'd lost, and an adolescent boy who had risen from the dead after drowning in the ocean. In each scene the boy was shirtless, his emerging sexuality shining from his narrow hips, exposed navel, and bare chest. She tried having the boy be the son of the husband and wife and then just made him a kid the couple met at the beach. She tried writing a scene where the woman kissed the boy, the man watching and then tried having the man kiss the boy, the woman watching. None of it worked. She began to actually feel the characters' impatience.

That evening Lisa made a fire in the fireplace and ate a bowl of brown rice. Clearly she was atoning for some sin, but which one? Since leaving the arts center, she hadn't returned to visit Joy. Seven months ago Joy had given birth as a gestational surrogate for friends of hers from college, Marisa and Eugene, who had intended to include Joy in their family, but over time grew possessive of the baby and began to exclude her. Lisa feared Joy's grief.

She poured fresh water from the spring into a glass and drank it, then drank another glass and looked out the window, seeing nothing but her own reflection. The fire in the hearth was making her skin dry and tight. A vertical wrinkle cut the center of her forehead. She no longer qualified as fresh and pretty and full of potential.

Still, she had to live. She changed into a silk shirt, tight jeans, stylish boots, and a man's tweed overcoat. Never mind the actual man, she told herself, whose cologne she imagined she could still smell on the coat. Larry. Never mind if Larry was still in the city, or if he had returned to the Midwest town of his birth, as he had said he was going to do, to find a woman with whom he could build a life that didn't revolve around anxiety, artistic ambition, and alcohol. It was tempting to wear a scarf for warmth, but Lisa knew the arts center would be full of women in scarves, so she pulled her hair up, decided against antique earrings, and left her neck bare and cold.

In the sky above the arts center, the white clouds in the black sky appeared fixed. Lisa parked her truck in the same spot she had used that morning to get water. The painters should be out here painting, she thought, but instead they're inside the arts center, getting toasted on free wine. She wondered if she would see Joy, or if Joy would be hiding in her room.

The first studio Lisa entered contained an installation of creepy fabric children. The children were bigger and less babyish than Cabbage Patch kids, but the effect was similar. They stood or sat in groupings, the way kids might on a playground, but each tableau had the feeling of a bad dream, perhaps because real kids never stood still. Some were missing an arm or leg. Others were crying. The books thrown at their feet were torn. The lighting was dim. Several women in their early twenties wearing short stretchy black skirts lingered, examining the dolls. Of course they could tell Lisa was older. Most likely they weren't even seeing her.

Being back in the arts center reminded Lisa of the creative, super-charged energy she'd felt when she'd lived here. It had felt as though everyone was constantly investigating everyone else, considering the possibility of cheating on their boyfriends or girlfriends, husbands or wives, of leaving their real lives temporarily behind. The question, *Will I have sex with you tonight?* rumbled beneath every interaction. The answer for her was always no.

After Larry left she'd grown used to being alone. It felt like she was storing things up, not to talk about, like she used to do, but to think about, or maybe write about. Was she in fact writing a play? Maybe she was merely having a deep and confusing conversation with herself.

The studio contained a window with a view into the still-dead garden, where a twenty-foot rough wood sculpture lit by spotlights sat in the snow. The sculpture's shape was reminiscent of a roller coaster. It also reminded Lisa of the Matchbox racetracks she and Therese had built and destroyed as children. Two of the guys she'd met at the spring this morning, Karl and Mateo, were throwing a glow-in-the-dark football between the curving pieces of wood. They were taking their game seriously, one or the other frequently diving to the ground to complete a difficult catch. Mateo chucked the ball, and instead of it carving through various empty spaces, it hit the wood, bounced off, and disappeared into a clump of bushes. Karl jumped through the sculpture and tackled Mateo. They rolled over and over through the snow.

Lisa left the installation and entered the central reception area, where the young men had matted hair and the older men ponytails and gray beards. The women were, many of them, wearing scarves. Two fifty-ish women with stylishly short hair and geometric earrings were engaged in an animated conversation punctuated with laughter.

"That's so funny!"

"That's so true!"

A long narrow table was covered with white cloth, bottles of wine, and a platter of artisanal cheeses. Lisa was happy to find a real glass among the plastic ones. She was aware of constantly shopping, searching, hoping that whatever she found would fit, would be satisfying, would reflect well upon her. She knew she thought about men this way too, but in that case, she was also hoping to be chosen. What she didn't know was whether she was too much of a bargain or overpriced. Something wasn't right.

She cut a creamy hunk of cheese, spread it on a cracker, and ate it. She poured herself a glass of cold white wine, held the stem, and did not take a sip, leaving the reception area to enter another studio where a series of black and white photographs hung on the walls. The subject of each photograph was identical, the hindquarters of horses. Lisa tried to think of the subject in a different way, but the same words, the hindquarters of horses, kept repeating in her brain. She felt bad for the photographer, but not too bad, because there were small red stickers on several of the labels near the photographs, indicating they had sold.

In another studio people were gathered at the edges of the room looking at a man standing in the center of it. Lit candles were rigged onto a contraption on the ceiling above him and wax dripped onto his hair. Bicycle wheels were scattered across the floor. Lisa recalled the complex games she'd played as a child. Escape from the Nazis. Pioneers in a Snowstorm. She and Therese had made rafts and forts, schools and offices. Adults who made art were simply people who continued playing. The hot wax? The pain? She and Therese had ritually tested limits, sometimes pulling each other's hair, once even burning each other with matches. The matches had been her idea, but Therese had gone along with it.

The man in the red vest stood at Lisa's elbow. Sean.

"What do you think of this guy?" he asked quietly, tilting his head toward the man with the waxy hair.

Lisa looked at the golden wine in her glass instead of answering. "Tell me about your work."

"I hammer wood with two other morons." Sean took a sip from a bottle of beer. "Our assemblages shoot for mysterious complexity and always just miss."

Lisa smelled beer while he spoke, the odor having for her an extremely male, extremely attractive connotation. She moved closer, so their shoulders touched.

"You write plays?" asked Sean. "Why not books? Or movies?"

"That's like asking why you aren't a photographer."

"What would I photograph?"

"The hind quarters of horses?"

He grinned, and she felt both mean and successful making this joke.

"I'm writing a play about a teenage boy who drowns in the ocean one day and is on the beach the next."

Sean was watching her face as she spoke, either listening, or waiting for her to stop talking.

"Come see these paintings," he said. "This work is truly great."

She followed him into an expansive gallery of large and small paintings she recognized immediately as Joy's.

Joy was standing in the center of the gallery in a yellow dress meant for summer. On her feet were architectural sandals. Late in her pregnancy, her feet had swelled. During this time Lisa had gone with her upstate to see two dancers perform in a river. Insects swirled in the floodlights. Lisa stood with the rest of the audience on the muddy riverbank. Joy commandeered a giant rock, reaching around her belly to scratch the itchy tops of her feet. The dancers wore white robes, their black hair streaming behind them. The piece was so slow, so still, that when the male dancer lost his footing and floated back a foot or two in the current, the audience gasped. Tonight was not the first time Lisa wondered whether the performance in the river had been a bad omen, a lesson she as yet did not understand, or simply a modern dance.

"Lisa!" Joy said, opening her arms. "It's so good to see you!" Joy was skinny again, cropped black hair highlighting her cheekbones.

Lisa handed her wine to Sean. Joy held tightly to Lisa's elbows, pulled her close, spoke into her ear. "What are you doing with booze and a boy?"

"These are wonderful paintings," said Lisa, kissing Joy firmly on the cheek before breaking free. "You've been through so much. I expected your new work to be unrecognizable."

"Ha," said Joy. "I'm the same."

Only better, thought Lisa, and tried to recast the stab she felt in her chest as something more generous than jealousy. "Joy, this is Sean," said Lisa. "Sean, this is Joy."

"I didn't know you'd know each other," said Sean. "Wow. What a great show."

"I've seen you around," said Joy, "with a couple other guys?"

"Yeah," said Sean, and began to explain the philosophy of his collective.

Lisa drifted over to a corner of the gallery, where on a pedestal a book had been placed. The book contained sentence after sentence— whole paragraphs— of praise and admiration for the nuance, energy, intelligence, lush explosive color, technique, emotional complexity— including surprise— and many other wonderful aspects of Joy's work. Lisa turned to a blank page, wrote herself a note about the drowning boy, ripped the page out of the book, and stashed it in the pocket of her jeans. In the center of the gallery, other people had pushed past Sean, insulating Joy with congratulations and compliments. Lisa retrieved her wine.

Sean placed his hand on Lisa's back. His fingers felt strong, perhaps from hammering. "Want to hang out in my room?"

"And do what?"

After a moment of silent staring, Sean took her elbow and led her outside to a narrow, well-trodden channel through the snow.

The night felt colder. Lisa looked up to see the clouds replaced by the moon and stars. Sean kept his eyes on the path. The way he walked struck Lisa as dogged, determined. Not a drop of wine spilled when she wedged the glass into a pile of snow near the door Sean held open. She followed him up a flight of stairs, down a hallway, and through a door he pushed open with his elbow, as if afraid of germs on the knob. Three unmade beds lined the wall. Along the other wall were tall windows without shades or curtains.

"They make you sleep here together?"

"We requested it from the point of view of the collective. Did I mention we're a bunch of idiots?" Now this grin of his was almost gentle.

From the window, the sculpture, Karl, Mateo, and their glowing football were still visible. Lisa was sure that the game of catch was part of their art, and wondered if the collective had had to reach consensus on Sean not participating. She wondered if they knew where he was, and what he was doing. He didn't light a candle or offer her some pot. He found an old metal key on top of a dresser and locked the door. The light from the window—the snow reflecting the moon—made the room bright. He was so young. Sometimes Lisa wished she wasn't as smart as she was, or at least could be better at denial. She wanted a reason to drink and was willing to look for a sign from the universe. After this—whatever this was with Sean—was over, she would retrieve her glass from the snow. If the wine hadn't frozen, she would drink it.

Sean moved toward her, his hands on her neck just warm enough.

Family Leave

LIKE MANY people in the financial services industry, Mark had no savings; he agreed to buy life insurance only after Aleksandar's adoption was complete. Because the policy had been so recently signed and the cause of death overdose, the insurance company refused to pay.

Therese climbed into bed and picked up *The New Yorker* she'd bought earlier along with more over-the-counter sleeping pills, a pregnancy test, and a bag of Hershey's kisses. In her thirty-eight years on the south shore of Long Island, the only person she could recall ever reading *The New Yorker* was her sister Lisa.

Therese read the comics and poems and two long articles, one about the artist Andy Goldsworthy, the other about the writer Ayn Rand.

"I'm like Ayn Rand," Therese remarked, though she was alone, and other than being generally thought of as a bitch, she was nothing like Ayn Rand: different politics, different preoccupations, different haircut.

Mark was the opposite of Andy Goldsworthy. Andy Goldsworthy revered life in all its forms, patiently standing for hours in the sun, melting two icicles to form one horn. Mark had been a stockbroker, a drug addict.

The carpet around the bed was scattered with bits of silver foil from the kisses. Therese got up to take a sleeping pill and turn on the television before climbing back into bed and pulling up the covers. She woke up several hours later, her T-shirt wet, the sheets clammy, unsure whether she was sweating or crying. There's nothing worse than a wet T-shirt in bed, she thought, though she knew of many things worse. She put on Mark's flannel pajamas, sat in a chair in the living room, and looked out the window at the darkness. Her feet grew cold, even though it was late June. She retrieved a blanket and pillow from the linen closet and moved to the couch. Mark had been dead for three months.

"How are you going to afford your mortgage if you don't go back to work?" Therese was repeating out loud the question first asked by her boss, an abrasive defense attorney. In fact, on her paralegal salary alone she would not be able to pay the mortgage, but without a job she would not be able to even rent an apartment and would be forced to move back in with her parents.

After preschool the following afternoon, Adam, Mark's father, was waiting on the sidewalk in front of Therese's house in the shade, stooping beneath the branches of trees.

"Pop-pop's here." In the rearview mirror, Therese watched Aleksandar take his thumb out of his mouth. She had been his mother for only nine months. Prior to the adoption, he'd lived in an orphanage in Bulgaria.

"Pop-pop?" Aleksandar replaced his thumb.

"Yeah." She got out of the car, opened the rear door, and unbuckled his car seat.

"Pop-pop! Pop-pop!" Aleksandar jumped out of the car, ran to Adam, and hugged him around the knees.

Adam's face was Mark's face, but thirty years older. Mark's grin had been shifty. Adam's smile was weighted with grief. Like Mark, Adam was tall and thin. His long arms wrapping around Therese's shoulders felt as if Mark was reaching out from the land of the dead, which happened to smell like Pinaud Clubman aftershave.

"Miriam asked to see you," said Adam. Miriam's cancer had been making incremental progress for years. Chemo and radiation were no longer working. Mark died three months ago and his mother seemed determined to join him. His once-aloof father had begun to cling to Therese, often showing up, like today, unannounced.

"Okay, I'll visit Miriam," Therese said, whereupon Adam finally let go. "I'm going to make dinner." She led the way inside the house.

"Pop-pop, play cars!" Aleksandar ran to a pile of Matchbox cars on the living room rug. His orange shirt and blue shorts were the same colors as some of the vehicles.

Therese chopped onions in the kitchen. Typically she drank cold white wine while she cooked, but the habit seemed derelict with another adult in the vicinity. Plus it was three-thirty in the afternoon. Plus she was pregnant.

In the living room, Aleksandar was almost singing while he played with his grandfather. When content he emitted a nonstop musical tale about whatever he was doing; his song concerned the cars on the rug, what they were like, what they could and could not do.

In moments like these Therese derived her most intense pleasure from being a mother. She also enjoyed when Aleksandar looked at her directly, which happened only rarely. He seemed startled when he did, as if most of the time she belonged to his internal world.

She slid the knife under the chopped onions, transporting them to the olive oil in a pan on the stove. June wasn't deep enough into summer to turn on the air conditioner; a small amount of perspiration didn't bother her.

"So you'll go see Miriam tomorrow?" Adam stood in the doorway to the kitchen, holding Aleksandar upside down by the ankles, Aleksandar red-faced, ecstatic, his hands scrabbling toward but not reaching the linoleum.

"Tomorrow I have an appointment." Therese pushed the onions around the pan with a spoon. Neither Miriam's terminal illness nor Mark's death had changed the fact that her brain was rutted with resentment of her mother-in-law.

"Go the day after." Adam lowered Aleksandar until Aleksandar walked his hands forward on the linoleum. "Don't wait too long."

When Adam let go of Aleksandar's feet, Aleksandar continued across the kitchen floor on his hands and knees.

"Will you stay for dinner?" asked Therese. She pretended not to hear the undertones of her request-masked-as-invitation: neediness, loneliness, sexuality. A man and woman alone. Aleksandar meowed. Almost alone.

"I can't," said Adam. "Miriam's nurse will soon be leaving for the evening." He opened his arms for a good-bye hug.

With her head on Adam's chest, Therese began to sweat in earnest. She imagined Adam removing her clothes. Another fantasy was to punch and keep punching him. During his embrace, a few golden onions fell from her spatula onto the floor. Aleksandar crawled over, meowing, to eat them.

In the morning Therese took Aleksandar to preschool and then drove to the Lawnhurst Motel, a white two-storied building with external stairs and halls.

Before entering the appointed room, she looked across Sunrise Highway to the trestle of the Long Island Rail Road.

Mark had taken the train into the city every weekday morning. It took time to get from the village of Lawnhurst to Penn Station to Wall Street, or from Wall Street to Penn Station back to Lawnhurst. Most often the time was predictable, but sometimes the LIRR and all the roads and tunnels into and out of the city became more complicated than the typical rush hour.

When there was a train workers' strike.

When there was a heavy snowstorm.

When there was a hurricane.

When the towers were hit.

When there was a mechanical failure with the trains or the tracks.

When there was a blackout or brownout.

When there was a bomb threat.

"Therese?" Jude stood inside the room, holding the door open. He looked like he'd gained weight, maybe as much as twenty pounds. Had she knocked without realizing it? Everything in the room but the brown furniture and carpet was white and worn: the walls, the ceiling, the bedspread, the lampshades.

Jude was neither as tall nor straightforwardly handsome as Mark had been, but he was wry, sensual. His lips were almost too big, his grey eyes too intelligent. Mark's oldest friend. They had all known one another since high school. She hadn't seen him since the funeral mass. He'd left before it was over; they hadn't spoken until she'd called him a day ago and they'd made the plan to meet.

He pulled a pint of Jack Daniels from his blazer pocket and placed it on top of the television.

Therese went into the bathroom for two glasses, the tops covered in paper. She set the glasses next to the bottle and sat down next to Jude at the end of the bed, facing the mirror that hung over the low bureau.

In the mirror she examined Jude's black T-shirt, his black blazer, his hair, greying at the temples and cut more severely than usual, as if to compensate for the extra pounds. Therese saw her curls beginning to frizz. Her knit dress clung; her breasts did look bigger.

"We don't have to come here anymore," said Jude.

"It didn't occur to me to meet you at my house," said Therese. "But we could."

"That's not what I meant." Jude's palm slid down her spine.

The ancient air conditioner lodged in the window made a stuttering sound. Her anticipation felt muted, but the craving beneath it was as strong as ever. There had always been other men, but Jude was her original. Her affair with him ran alongside her marriage to Mark; now it would continue past it. She hadn't had a sexual interaction of any kind, not in person, not by phone, not by e-mail, in the three months since Mark's death. She stood up and turned to face Jude. He stood to remove her dress, her bra, her underwear, and sat back down at the end of the bed. She knelt in front of him, unzipped his pants and began to give him a mechanical blow job.

"I can't." Jude pushed away, lay flat.

The lack of climax made the transaction feel worthless.

"I'm taking a shower," said Therese, as if that could help.

"T," said Jude when she emerged from the bathroom, one meager towel wrapped around her body and another around her hair, though her hair wasn't wet; as she neared forty she found that if she washed it too often it grew brittle. Jude had moved both pillows to his side of the bed and tucked them behind his back. He was still fully clothed, his feet bare. He gestured toward the bureau, where one of the glasses was half-filled with amber liquor. The glass on his bedside table had been drained.

"Did you find us a movie?" asked Therese. They usually watched a black and white one before Jude took the train back into the city. He worked freelance and could come and go as he pleased.

"We're not watching a movie!" Jude jumped off the bed, began to pace. "You're acting like nothing has changed, Therese. How are you? How's your little boy?"

Instead of answering, Therese refilled Jude's glass. He knew even less than she did about children. It was interesting. Now that she knew she was pregnant, everything about her body confirmed it: not just the lack of a period and swollen breasts; her stomach more round than flat, her face full, her fingernails strong. She was hungry all the time, woke up each morning thinking of food. She was excited about being pregnant, but it felt like a betrayal. She and Mark had tried for years.

"Therese? We need to talk about Mark."

The baby wasn't Mark or Jude's.

And it was too hard to explain to Jude that Mark—at least in her head, she wasn't insane, she knew the difference—Mark absolutely did not feel gone. He felt out, the way he did when he was running some errand they both pretended wasn't about buying cocaine. But in this case, as she knew he wasn't actually buying cocaine or doing anything worrisome that she should be trying to prevent instead of—since denial wasn't really possible—acquiescing, his absence felt more okay than it usually did.

"Aleksandar is fine," she told Jude.

Jude shook his head.

"Nothing has to change," she said, knowing immediately how stupid and wishful she sounded.

"Mark was my best friend."

"Everyone felt that way about Mark," she snapped. It was true. Mark had had that effect on people; it's what made him a good stockbroker, a good salesman. People trusted him. They felt Mark liked them. And they were right. Mark liked everyone but himself.

"We can't keep doing this!" Jude was standing next to the bed with his hands on his hips. An indignant Jude was completely unprecedented, borderline funny.

"Why? Because now I'm free and we could actually be together? Or are you punishing me for cheating on your friend?" Therese removed the towel from her hair. She wondered what Jude would say if she told him she was pregnant.

"Fine, I call your bluff." Jude downed his drink. Looked her in the eye. "I love you."

"Don't say it if it isn't true."

"Please, Therese, I've been your tit for tat, your little reward, your escape valve."

"No you haven't."

"Then what has this been?" Jude gestured to the room and Therese saw it clearly. This place they had used on and off for almost twenty years, shabby and hard. "I know you love me too." Flat statement of fact.

"You know I don't care about love." Therese watched as Jude let this declaration roll off. No softness remained in the carpet they stood on, or in any aspect of the room; even the towel pressed against her body felt gritty. "With you I feel unconfined. Which I like." She took off the towel and looked to see if her full naked body had any effect on Jude. His face didn't change but his new extra bulk, this transformation from lithe to almost stocky, felt as though he was beefing up, preparing for something. "What have you been getting out of it?" She wanted to say something to make Jude flinch but instead he was impassive.

"I liked knowing I would see you, and then seeing you," said Jude. "I liked knowing you wouldn't want anything from me other than this." He gestured wryly to the room—acknowledging the dreariness too, whereas before they'd treated the shitty motel room as a kind of clubhouse. "I liked my limited role as your special friend." He grinned. Out popped old familiar I don't give a shit Jude. "And the sex."

Sex had always been Therese's attempt to feel more alive. Now she didn't want to feel anything, but sex could be good for that too.

"Please," she said, sliding beneath the sheets, holding out her hand.

Jude squeezed her forearm. "You need this?" His voice hovered between benevolence and violence; he climbed on top of her, his extra weight pressing her down into the mattress. "This is what you need?" He tugged the sheet out from between them. He might think he was being rough, but they had been together for so long he was her other husband.

Later that afternoon Therese arrived home from preschool with Aleksandar to see her parents' car parked in front of her house. Like Adam, her parents often dropped by unannounced to investigate: was the widow still intact?

Unlike Adam, they did not wait out front. They'd kept the key she'd given them after Mark died, when for several days and nights they'd stayed with her. It felt ungrateful to ask them to return it, though she felt invaded.

"Grandma and Grandpa are here."

Aleksandar didn't respond. He'd been quiet the entire way home.

Therese tried and failed to remember if he'd been silent the other afternoons she had spent with Jude, or another man who wasn't Mark. She got out of the car, opened the back door, and unlatched the restraints on Aleksandar's seat.

"Come on," she prompted. "Let's go."

They walked up the steps to the house side by side. Aleksandar did not insist on opening the front door.

"We were wondering when you'd get here." Therese's mother, Alice, was sitting on the couch, *The New Yorker* on the cushion next to her.

Therese tried to remember if she'd brought the magazine into the living room. Had her mother been snooping around in her bedroom? What about the wastebasket in her bathroom?

"Hello there." Her father, Paul, was sitting in Mark's chair, reading *Newsday*. Aleksandar walked over and stood at his knee while he pulled a roll of multicolored Life Savers from his pocket. Aleksandar peeled one off and put it in his mouth. "Let's read the comics," said Therese's father. Aleksandar crawled onto his lap.

"Doesn't it make you crazy that your sister still doesn't know about your husband?" asked her mother. "It's unbelievable. It's unacceptable. Lisa is doing nothing to help you."

This was how they proceeded in her family: her mother waged war against the unfairness of life while her father remained close by, protecting no one but himself. A perpetual eye infection made the rim of his left lower lid red.

"Do you want coffee?" asked Therese.

"No thank you," said her father.

"It's too late in the day for coffee," said her mother.

"I'll make decaf," said Therese.

Her mother sighed impatiently.

The retreat to the kitchen felt cowardly and smart. Therese looked out the window while the coffee brewed; the forsythia had been in bloom when Mark died. Its yellow flowers were gone, the branches covered with green leaves. The leaves were oval-shaped, the edges jagged. She brought two cups of decaf into the living room.

"Obviously I failed with Lisa," said her mother. "But what did I do exactly? Is her life my fault?"

Therese's father continued reading the comics out loud to Aleksandar, saying "Ha ha ha," at each unfunny ending.

"Doesn't Lisa know we were all hurt as children? When I was a girl, the nuns hit our knuckles with rulers. We were told we were stupid. We were told not to speak. We were told we smelled. We were told we were ugly." Her mother sipped the decaf, making a face at the taste. Like many excellent attorneys, her technique was oblique and unrelenting.

Therese imagined an apt closing statement for her mother's bottom-line argument: In conclusion, Your Honor, we have all suffered, so no one can be blamed.

"How was preschool, Aleksandar?" Therese's father wore a half-smile that almost acknowledged changing the subject.

Aleksandar stuck out his tongue to display his thinning Life Saver.

"Don't do that," said Therese. "You had fun at school today, didn't you? Tomorrow is his last day for the year; it's a short day. He goes for just a couple of hours for the end of the year party. And that's it."

"Did you decide when you're going back to work?" Her mother put her cup down on the coffee table. "You know we'll take care of Aleksandar for you. But a little notice would help us plan."

"I know," said Therese. All the years of effort it had taken to become independent from her parents had become meaningless the moment Mark died. Boom: she needed them.

"Lisa hasn't contacted you, has she?" asked her mother.

"She has not." Therese knew this visit was basically another errand on her mother's list of things to do, like buying bread and returning library books. They all knew Lisa wasn't truly missing. Her time at the arts center in Vermont, where she'd gone to write a new play, had indeed ended, and she hadn't yet returned to New York. True, the emails they'd sent to her had bounced back, and her cell phone had been disconnected. It was irritating and worrisome and, yes, the timing sucked, but it was not without precedent.

Lisa had a history of secluding herself in order to write, as well as a history of drinking, and also a history of things never going as well as she wanted them to go. How could they? Lisa lived in what Therese thought of as La-La-Land. Lisa wanted total freedom. She wanted a man to love her for her quote unquote true self. She wanted artistic and financial fulfillment. It was more than wanted. Lisa felt she deserved these things. These things were her due.

"Lisa isn't thinking about anyone but herself." Her mother stood up.

"Ma, it takes time to write a play." It felt very sister-like defending Lisa, even though Therese had been thinking essentially the same thing.

"Lisa could write in the city. She has her own apartment. She doesn't have a real job. She doesn't have kids. She doesn't even have a boyfriend."

"She's going to feel bad enough when she finally comes home or gets in touch, and finds out what happened," said Therese. At least Lisa wasn't trying to fuck herself into existence, or obliterate herself that way. Lisa was trying to write herself into being, which seemed more constructive, more confident, at least less slutty. "You don't need to rub it in."

"I'm not rubbing it in."

Therese knew that what galled their mother most was someone in the family missing out on family pain when the rest of them were forced to endure it.

"Your father and I just came by to see how you and Aleksandar were doing. And to see if you were any closer to making a decision about going back to work."

"Did I tell you?" asked Therese. "Miriam isn't well. There's a hospice nurse." This was the smartest way to respond to her mother: to answer pain with pain. Though her mother frowned, Therese could see that this news about Miriam had a soothing effect.

"Oh dear," said her mother. "That is sad. Well, we've got to run."

Her father lifted Aleksandar from his lap and placed the newspaper on the coffee table. Therese opened the front door. Outside, a robin trilled in one of the trees.

"Summer is here," said her mother. "I hope it doesn't get too hot." She picked up *The New Yorker* from the couch. "Are you finished with this? There's a calendar in there. If you don't need us to watch Aleksandar, your father and I are planning to go a museum in the city one day next week."

"Take it." Therese knew neither words nor art would be her salvation. Religion was obviously out. She'd thought her power was her beauty—in the mirror on the back of the bathroom door in the motel, her knees looked ugly, caved in on the sides—but the rest of her was ripening— beauty was surface. Beneath was the power of physicality.

"Maybe you and Aleksandar can come with us," said her father, kissing Aleksandar.

"Probably not." Her mother waved the magazine rolled in her fist. "Therese and Aleksandar are usually busy."

"Aleksandar, say good-bye to Grandma Alice and Grandpa Paul," said Therese.

She didn't want to go into the city to look at art with her parents. Nonetheless, the non-invitation stung. She was also disappointed that her mother—who always acted all-knowing—had not divined her pregnancy.

Though Therese locked the door behind them, her parents still had their key.

Aleksandar's preschool was demarcated into a variety of spaces: sand and water tables, a pillowed reading nook, a cardboard block area, shelves of puzzles and magnets, a dress-up box, a kitchen, which also included dolls and cribs, and the snack table, where the three-to-four-year-olds were taught to smear cream cheese across bagels all by themselves using mini knives.

Life was really like that, people moving from one place and activity to another, utilizing specialized tools and materials.

The preschoolers, however, thought Therese, bending down to give Aleksandar a kiss good-bye at the door, had an advantage. When one of them had a meltdown, which often occurred despite the age-appropriate toys and activities, the teacher would sit cross-legged on the floor, the distraught child in her lap, and rock and pat the child's back until he or she was ready to rejoin the group. Grown-ups had to learn to self-soothe.

Therese drove to Mark's parents' house. On the way, she replayed one of many conversations she had had with Mark about his mother before they were married. In this particular conversation, Mark had told her that Miriam was upset because Therese wouldn't convert to Judaism.

"Is she out of her mind?" Therese remembered yelling. She and Mark had been sitting in a booth at a diner, sharing a plate of onion rings. "I quit being Catholic! Why would I become Jewish? I don't believe in any of that shit!"

"You don't have to go crazy," said Mark. "What I do is ignore her." He bit into an onion ring. Part of the onion slithered out and landed in the puddle of ketchup on the plate. He fished the onion out and placed it into Therese's mouth. "You take your mother and my mother way too seriously. My suggestion is, don't."

At the time Therese did not know why she had found this advice so annoying, but now she knew: one day, she too would become an unattractive old woman everyone alternately resented and ignored.

She parked behind the landscaping truck in front of Miriam and Adam's house. Mark had grown up in the old neighborhood in Lawnhurst, but as his parents grew richer they'd moved to a larger house in a wealthier section of town. Two stocky men were blowing grass clippings from the sidewalk. Adam's car was not in the driveway. Therese knocked, rang the bell, waited, removed the key from under the mat, and unlocked the door.

"Miriam?" she called softly. "Hello?" She couldn't remember the name of the hospice nurse. "It's Therese."

There was no answer. Perhaps the nurse was in the bathroom or on the phone. Perhaps it had been a difficult night and everyone was sleeping.

The front door opened directly into the living room. The objects here were not neutral. The television in the corner, the heavy drapes blocking the daylight, the couch where Therese had sat watching MTV with Mark when they had been in high school, her hands burrowing under his sweatshirt and jeans on the occasions when no one else was home.

Therese walked through the kitchen to get to Miriam's hospital bed in a back room. The vibration of the old refrigerator filled the room with sound. The kitchen table, normally covered by various boxes of crackers, browning bananas, and cans of Ensure, was shiny and bare. Therese listened for the sound of a toilet flushing, for clothes being loaded into the washer in the basement, for pills being counted and sorted into a sectional container, but heard nothing.

She fully expected Miriam's room to be empty, the IV pole bare, the hospital bed stripped, the blankets folded and stacked on a chair. It made sense. The hospice nurse and Adam weren't here. She was too late; Miriam was gone.

No, Miriam was in bed, hooked to an IV drip. Bottles of medicine cluttered her bedside table. She opened her eyes.

Therese sat down in the chair next to the bed, surprised to feel a rush of relief. "No one answered the door, so I used the spare key."

"My nurse got a call," said Miriam, her voice rough. "Her kid threw up at school. Too many cupcakes. Adam had to go somewhere. I don't remember."

"Aleksandar is having a party at school today too." The leather bag Therese held on her lap had the weight and warmth of a baby, and she dreamed for a moment she was holding baby Aleksandar. Impossible; he'd spent his first four years at the orphanage in Plovdiv. "How are you, Miriam?"

Miriam didn't respond. She had never been interested in social niceties; it was one of the qualities they shared.

"I should have invited a rabbi to Mark's wake," said Therese. "I know you wanted me to."

"There never should have been a wake," said Miriam.

At the wake Therese had stared at the light shining through Miriam's white hair, but instead of compassion or sympathy, her heart was sealed in hate.

"I'm sorry," said Therese.

"Too late."

"Adam told me you wanted to see me."

"My question is, why are people so boring? They all do the same dumb things. These high school kids who cut themselves. Who started that? One stupid kid with a razor blade and now they all do it. Or the girls who don't eat."

Usually Miriam was so tight-lipped. High on medication, she reminded Therese of Mark when he was stoned, or Lisa when she was drunk, when things trapped inside began leaping or dribbling out.

"You carried on with other men," said Miriam. "Mark had his drugs."

Do you want to know which came first? Therese thought, but didn't say.

"You thought I hated you," said Miriam. "You weren't good for Mark. You didn't help him. Being with you made him worse."

Is this really necessary? Therese wanted to ask, but she knew it was.

"You have a boy now," said Miriam. "Wait. This will happen to you. I'm dying. I'm joining my son. You won't be there, but I don't feel good about it." Miriam shut her eyes and waved her pale hand as if to say, I'm done, now get out of here.

"God, Miriam." Therese stood up to go. "I'm pregnant."

"*Mazel tov.*" Was Miriam grimacing or trying to smile? Therese debated relating that the father was Kevin. But Miriam shut her eyes; she was breathing as if asleep.

Therese stood up and told herself to go—she had plenty to do. She needed to call her boss to discuss the details of returning to work, and then she needed to call her mother to ask her about taking care of Aleksandar. She needed to figure out when, exactly, she'd had her last period. But instead of leaving she sat back down, bag on her lap, and listened to Miriam snore until the hospice nurse returned.

When Therese woke to the sound of Aleksandar's voice the next morning, she remembered preschool was over for the year.

Aleksandar was in his room talking to his toys. Therese had arranged his bed so that when he wasn't asleep he could look out the window, but on the occasions when she watched him from the doorway she usually saw him curled toward the wall, talking to the toy in his hand, a metal car or wooden animal.

As she listened to Aleksandar's voice, she heard something she knew she no longer had, nor could she pinpoint when she'd lost it.

At some point he would become aware of being hungry or thirsty, and this would break him out of his contentment, his engagement with his toy and his story-song, and make him get out of bed. He was young enough to believe that in this house food could only be obtained through her, though soon he would learn to go into the kitchen and find a bowl and spoon, the box of cereal. Soon he would be strong enough to pull open the refrigerator door and lift the milk.

She could hear him get out of bed and walk from his bedroom to hers. The house contained them. The walls and floors and ceilings gave them a place to be.

"Mom." He stood leaning against her bed.

She had heard of other children running to their parents' beds and jumping in, whether their parents were awake or welcoming, but Aleksandar never jumped.

"Come here." She lifted the blanket.

Aleksandar stretched out next to her, his feet reaching just past her knees. He smelled like strawberry jam. One night Mark had brought home a bag of plastic men attached with string to flimsy plastic parachutes. One by one they'd been knotted or lost. Aleksandar clasped the only one left. He held the man above their heads until he could no longer stand it, and with a shriek he let him go.

The Dogs

BEFORE HE fell asleep Aleksandar experienced the sensation of wood he associated with popsicles, the flat side and the thick side of the stick. It was almost a dream, but he wasn't asleep.

His mind felt strange and floating. It wasn't like during the day when his mother or teacher or grandmother was talking to him and making him talk, pointing at a block and saying "red" until he repeated "red" and then at another block and saying "green" until he repeated "green." They did this with numbers and letters too, and with objects: "shirt," "pants," "sneakers," "car," "fork," "spoon," and on and on, the days a river of words he must repeat, "cow," "sheep," "chicken," "horse," "dog," "cat," to make his mother and his teacher and his grandmother's faces alive.

Sometimes they tested him, holding up or pointing to the thing they wanted him to say and if he forgot, their faces looked dead. Sometimes at home he sat on his mother's lap with a book while she pointed at a page full of faces.

"Happy," she said, pointing at the line of the mouth turned up like the bottom of a boat, and he repeated "happy."

"Sad," she said, pointing at the face where the boat was upside down. "Sad," he repeated.

Tonight his dogs were jammed between the wall and his bed where he'd jammed them, where he jammed them every night, trapping them so they would be there again in the morning. In the morning he would decide whether to take them out and kiss and hug them or leave them mashed and barely breathing. He wasn't sure if they were dead until he touched them. When he touched them he could tell they were alive.

Some nights he jammed them against the wall and pulled them out repeatedly.

We're only kidding, said the kids at school, holding their nose when he came close, saying PU, PU, and then, Don't tell, we're only kidding, don't be a baby.

Now he pulled the first dog out and felt how sad the other one was to maybe be dead. He pulled out the second dog too.

"Only kidding," he whispered as he set them on his chest. "Be happy."

Because it was dark he couldn't see their tan bodies or dark brown ears, but he could see both colors in his mind as he ran his hands down their backs. He wanted the weight of their bodies on his own body to weigh much more.

"You," he whispered in a voice he could barely hear, "are very good." The bodies of the dogs were long and skinny; they were on their bellies, the tips of their noses rested at his collarbones, their tails ended at the bottom of his ribcage. He pressed their boneless bodies down against his own, his hands continuing downward to the bones of his hips rising like mountains in the dark room.

The longest finger on each hand was in the middle. He pressed the middle finger down as hard as he could against his upper thighs, and then all the fingers down. He wanted to see if he could hurt himself but he never could.

His hands moved from his hips to what he thought of as the center, as if he was a star stretching out in all directions, or if he was a jellyfish, or a flower, or a circle made of paper, or a cookie. He rubbed his hands over the center. His mother called his thing *penis*. At the home they said don't touch it. His mother never said don't. It was soft now but when he woke in the morning it was hard, and if he rubbed it hardened. It was funny sticking up.

He moved his hands so his palms again lay on his hipbones. He pushed his hands over the bones like the plastic men who fit on plastic horses, their molded legs. The dogs panted against his neck.

At first he had not wanted to be in his room alone at night.

Mark used to sit next to his bed in a chair. Then Mark was dead in the box in the room full of people. Then Mark was buried in the box in a hole in the grass.

He was forgetting Mark, he was forgetting the home, Mark and the people from the home sliding away like a wave, rushing away to somewhere else, though there were pictures of the home in the book his mother showed him: his wooden crib against a wall next to other cribs, tables pushed together and children pushed up to the table in chairs with long legs. In another book his mother showed him pictures of Mark, of himself in Mark's arms, and sitting on Mark's lap.

"Your daddy," she said, pointing. "He loved you so much. I'm sorry he's gone. You have a birth daddy and a birth mommy too, but we don't have a picture of them. They loved you very very much, but they couldn't take care of you, even though they wanted to, so they gave you to the home, and the home gave you to me and daddy. Your birth parents and the people at the home wanted you to be safe and happy. They knew we would take good good care of you and love you very, very much."

Aleksandar wondered who had told her to say these words.

There was no time he remembered before the time at the home. He could see from the pictures at the home he had never been alone there.

At first he did not like this house, this bed, this room, the darkness.

"Night light," he had learned to say when Mark sat in the chair, but now he said, "Turn it off."

"Are you sure?" his mother asked at first until each night she turned off the light and shut the door.

Aleksandar took his hands from his hips and brought them back to the dogs. He pinched their tails until they yipped, pinched harder until they cried, then stroked their backs until they squirmed against his chest with contentment.

If he was a Life Saver there were would be an empty space in the middle of his body, the space his tongue always went, his mouth filled with spit, the flavor of the candy growing larger as the candy grew thinner, the hole larger, the sensation of the ring in his mouth changing from round to flat to sharp, like the popsicles he licked and sucked. At first they were so frozen he couldn't taste them and he scraped his front teeth across the tops to generate a mound of icy shavings, and used his teeth to push the mound to the center of his tongue where it melted and he could taste the sugar.

At school on the playground another boy showed him how to scrape a popscicle stick against the blacktop until it sharpened into a knife. The boy stabbed him in the arm and he'd taken the stick and stabbed the boy. The boy yelled and the teacher came over and took the knife and made them sit in chairs where they pretended to be sad.

Aleksandar kept a plastic baggie of pretzels under his bed. Most of the pretzels were broken and on the way to becoming salty dust. There was also a sleeve of saltines back against the wall. Two oranges were shriveling in his closet. His mind journeyed to each of these caches. His attempts to save candy never succeeded; he could not resist eating it as soon as it was given to him, just as he could not resist begging for more. Most people could say no at least sometimes. Pop Pop could say no, but Grandpa Paul could not. The dogs wanted some pretzels.

"No," Aleksandar told them, mashing them back into the space between his bed and the wall, filling the hole with their long skinny bodies.

Hamartia

THE NIGHT Miriam lay dying Adam stepped from the room where Rose, the hospice nurse, checked Miriam's pulse.

PLEASE COME OVER he texted his daughter-in-law, Therese. Mark's widow.

A text was no place to say: Miriam's last breaths may be hurting *me* more than they're hurting her. And Adam knew how that sounded. He wished Miriam's labored breathing inspired compassion, but tonight reminded him, only far worse, of the nights one of them had had a hacking cough and the other, exhausted and irritated, finally went to sleep on the living room couch saying "I think *you'll* be more comfortable."

From the beginning he had conceptualized marriage as a long game—it turned out to be the longest—and strategized appropriately. He kept a tally, not niggling but accurate, of how much he gave and how much he received. He was sure Miriam had done the same; he was sure it was the key to their relatively successful marriage.

That was now ending after years of Miriam's illness. The sounds she was making wavered between snoring and choking.

BRING ALEKSANDAR WITH YOU. He wanted the boy in his arms.

I'm coming, Therese texted back. *No need to SHOUT.*

If, all those years ago, breast cancer had happened to Miriam alone, thought Adam, closing his eyes for a minute while leaning against the wall in the kitchen, she might have kept her mouth shut out of privacy or shame, but breast cancer happened to so many, and many women, not just Miriam, believed the groundwater on Long Island was to blame.

The women believed they should not be getting cancer, period, but especially not in such quantity: sisters and cousins and friends. Friends of friends. A neighbor down the block, a neighbor around the block. Women the next town over and the town after that. He'd watched the women's interpretation of breast cancer evolve over time. First they saw it as a private tragedy, then as a public health emergency, and later, a sign human beings had damaged mother earth.

Adam thought of breast cancer as his nemesis.

Therese arrived at his front door in shorts and cheap rubbery flip-flops. Pregnant women no longer wore flowing clothes; Therese's tank top clung to her belly. Her wild hair was caught back in a ponytail.

"Is Aleksandar in the car?"

"He's just four, Adam." Therese covered a yawn with her hand. "I dropped him off with my parents. How is Miriam?"

"Miriam is unconscious," said Adam. "Come in."

"I'm sorry, but I have to go home for a little while." Rose leaned down to retie the laces on her sneakers. Her nurse-clothes were soft; today she wore a gray t-shirt and sweatpants. "I have to check on my little one. He's with his sister—she's only twelve—he's started vomiting. He's been running a fever." Rose tucked her blonde hair behind multiply-pierced ears. Adam guessed she was close to Therese's age, but solidified and strengthened by two children—she never mentioned a husband, or the children's father. Rose took more breaks than she should, but Adam tried to cut her some slack. "I live close," she assured Therese. "I'll be back in a half hour. Less. Miriam is resting comfortably."

Rose shut the door behind her. Miriam's labored breathing reached the foyer.

"She doesn't sound comfortable," said Therese.

"Listen, Therese." Adam opened his arms. "Move in here. I can take care of you. You and Aleksandar and the baby."

Therese put her hands on her hips.

Adam lowered his arms and Therese walked past him toward Miriam's room. Adam lifted a chair from the dining room and followed her, placing this chair next to the one already beside Miriam's bed, the one where Therese was now sitting and peering at her mother-in-law. Miriam's eyes were closed, her mouth slightly open. She was wearing what Adam thought of as a non-expression. When she wore that face, he knew it was enough already.

"She's in pain," said Therese.

"No." Adam pointed at the IV drip. "It's a high dose of morphine."

"Okay." Therese's voice was full of doubt. "She doesn't sound good."

Adam didn't want to say the words *death rattle*. He handed Therese the booklet Rose had given him.

"You want me to read this?"

He nodded; the booklet was about hospice, about the transition between life and death.

With Mark, Adam imagined, one moment he was alive, his body receiving an injection of cocaine and heroin, the next he was dead.

They'd told people half the truth—Mark had had a stroke. They didn't tell them the reason, though many people knew enough to guess correctly. The transition, if you could call it that, and Adam wouldn't, he'd call it doom without end, came later, when Adam saw Mark, his beloved child, an inert body in a coffin.

"They say you need to give Miriam explicit permission," murmured Therese, pointing at a page in the booklet. "She can let go if you tell her you're going to be okay. Have you done that?"

"I'll be okay if you and Aleksandar move in with me." It felt strange to be openly needy; he'd dispensed with vulnerability at a young age as it was never an effective strategy.

"Adam, please," said Therese, turning the page of the brochure, "I'm reading."

Adam didn't want to think about Mark, didn't want to think about all that had gone wrong. Adam managed life as well as he did by walling off whatever might cloud his vision or impede his objectives. Sure it was good for things like the Berlin Wall to come down, but he, an individual man, needed partitions in order to cope. At some point he'd accepted there was no point in struggling against the most difficult reality in his life: his son used heavy drugs. He couldn't change that fact, he could only contain it by choosing not to think about it.

Guilt was a waste of time.

Adam never felt guilty, for example, about being successful. Why shouldn't he provide for his family, and provide handsomely? His people had been persecuted for centuries. It's not like that was over and done with, either. And his family had had nothing; Miriam's family had had nothing; they both had come from nothing. Why shouldn't he make money? Why shouldn't he rise?

Only 9-11 had inspired the free-floating guilt of which so many people complained. He didn't have an office at the Trade Center, but went to meetings frequently in Tower One. He could easily have been there that morning at Cantor Fitzgerald, flirting with the receptionists, helping himself to a donut. Six hundred and fifty eight of their people killed, while a few blocks away he'd been sitting at his desk muttering over spreadsheets.

A friend—he'd lived through Auschwitz-Birkenau while his little brother perished—talked about survivor's guilt.

"It's always there." His usually brash friend shrugged submissively. "A coat I can't take off."

Adam watched as Therese continued to make a show of reading the pamphlet. The heat rising from his daughter-in-law's body was in direct contrast to the cooling body of his wife.

Throughout life man was tested to determine his mettle. What kind of man was he? What kind of choice would he make? Would he cling to death, to sorrow? Or would he reach out toward renewal, toward youth?

In her tank top and shorts, Therese looked like a kid.

When Mark was ten years old he turned into one of those twerps who enjoyed needling his parents. In middle school his class did a unit on stereotypes.

"Are all Jews rich?" he asked one night at dinner. "A kid kept asking that question."

Adam ignored him. Mark would learn it didn't matter what religion you were what race you were what your father did or didn't do. You got ahead by working harder and being smarter and more ruthless than the other guy. He feared his son had had it too easy to learn this. It was the kind of thing you had to learn the hard way. No one had been standing by waiting to hold Adam's hand and guide him gently out of Brooklyn; he'd fought his way out.

"That's what they're teaching you?" said Miriam. "I'm calling the principal tomorrow."

"Miriam," said Adam. "Relax. Mark, don't be an asshole. How could all Jews be rich if we're not rich—we're comfortable—and we're Jews? How could all Jews be rich if on one side your grandparents live in a moldy house in Midwood and the other lives in a one-bedroom apartment on Queens Boulevard? How can all Jews be rich if the mother of your friend David from Hebrew School is on Foodstamps?"

"He doesn't know about the Foodstamps." Miriam shook her head. "And the mold in your parents' house has been removed. You have a big mouth, you know that?"

Therese handed back the hospice brochure and stood up, the back of her thighs peeling away from the wooden chair.

"I have to pee. I'll be right back."

"Okay." Adam had the distinct feeling she was leaving to make a call or text someone, but who? Her sister Lisa was a lush and AWOL; her parents were asleep. Therese's infidelities had made Miriam furious and disgusted, but Adam didn't have a mother's blinding protectiveness. Therese's behavior made logical sense. If his son had a fatal flaw, his son's wife should have one, too. They'd never discussed it explicitly, of course, but he knew Miriam would have preferred Therese to be blameless and long suffering, which made no sense since Miriam was a feminist. Her "Sisterhood is Powerful" refrigerator magnet went up in the 70's and had never come down.

"Sisterhood is Powerful" is how Miriam had dealt with her cancer. She turned to other women who had it too—they all met and talked, they talked on the phone, they talked in person. These women who had breast cancer talked *a lot*. They were white women—Jews, Italians, Irish Catholics. They were Black women. They were Hispanic women. They were New Yorkers. The women of Miriam's generation were different from their mothers and grandmothers. Some had screamed and torn their clothes when the Beatles came to Shea. Some had gone to college. Some had met Bella Abzug or Angela Davis at a political rally or a march. They didn't have to be the girls who'd burned their bras while the boys burned their draft cards. Miriam said when it came to voting about it, most of them were pro-choice, even the Catholics.

"Even the Catholics?" Adam wasn't convinced.

"Okay, the smartest Catholics are pro-choice, no, the ones who are the kindest. Who wants to go back?" Miriam said to him. "Who wants to be responsible for another woman's brutalization?"

When it came to her own son, however, when it came to Therese, Miriam had made an exception. He didn't think Miriam wanted Therese to be subjected to evil—she just wanted Therese to be good, even when Mark was behaving badly. It was more than that. She wanted Therese to succeed where she had failed; she wanted Therese to save her son. But instead of admitting that, Miriam got angry. Not just at Therese—she blamed Therese's infidelities on her nature, which she attributed to her mother, Alice. If parental blame was to be placed, thought Adam, it should be placed on

Therese's father, Paul. He was weak and ineffective. Therese probably inherited her shortcomings from him.

Therese had been in the bathroom for such a long time Adam began to believe it was too traumatizing for her to be here witnessing Miriam's death so soon after Mark's. He should have thought of that before he called her.

Miriam's breathing was moving into a new pattern of stopping and starting. No, Miriam's breathing was mostly stopping. It was better for Miriam that Therese wasn't in the room. Miriam might just stubbornly hang on until she could die in private.

Adam took his wife's wasting hand. His felt like a claw.

"Miriam."

A month ago she had stopped wearing her engagement ring, her wedding ring, also the amethyst and the sapphire, because the rings kept falling off.

"You can go, Miriam. I'm going to live. I'm going to be okay."

Had her years of cancer prepared them for this? After the breast cancer came other kinds. Were decades of pain and treatment, the presence of death lingering at the edges better than dying suddenly from a drug-induced heart attack?

"Go if you need to go." He said it loudly so she could hear him.

Her eyelids moved.

Was she giving him a near-death version of her famous look? The one she gave him when he became, as she put it, "self-aggrandizing?"

After Mark died people oozed empathy. "It was so sudden" they all said, as if knowing beforehand could have helped.

"Which is it, Miriam? What's worse?"

Miriam was the drummer in their duo. She kept the beat, kept him from the pratfalls of hubris, cured him of casually mentioning his tax bracket, of over-tipping pretty waitresses, of insisting on picking up the tab when Mark took him out to dinner on his birthday.

"What's a better way to die, Miriam, fast or slow?" He wasn't imagining it. Miriam was removing her hand from his own.

Adam sat looking at his wife and remembering how good she was to everyone before she had become ill and for many years after: feeding people, listening to them, making them laugh. She had always been liberal in every way and he had always been fine with it. A mother should be generous and humane. A father's job was to make money. The way he saw it, his cutthroat competitiveness purchased her largesse. They rounded each other out. Not that Miriam had ever been a softie.

When Mark was an infant Miriam let him cry himself to sleep; she put him on a schedule for feeding. Early on she made him use the toilet, and wipe himself too. In kindergarten she made him eat his carrots before he could be excused from the dinner table. Every night his job was clearing the table and loading the dishwasher. After he was finished with that task Miriam would make him sponge down the dining room table, dry it with a dishtowel, and then unload his backpack onto the table and do his homework. Mark didn't rush to finish his homework in order to watch television because Monday through Thursday the television stayed off, no exceptions. If Adam wanted to watch a Knicks game, he went out to a bar.

They had wanted more children, not a passel like the

Catholics or the Hasidim, Jesus Christ, but at least two. Miriam didn't get pregnant again after Mark, however, and it wasn't for the lack of them trying, or enjoying themselves while so doing. Of course it was disappointing, but once they failed to have two, they wised up and realized how lucky they were to have one. Neither he nor Miriam were the types to be stupid, to be brokenhearted when they already had a healthy, intelligent child.

So the sadness turned into acceptance and gratefulness, though purity of emotion was one of the things Adam missed about being young—how singularly he had loved and hated and desired. As he grew older he learned how to even things out in order to sustain them, or survive them, but it also felt like everything got watered down.

He and Miriam focused on the positive: not having another child meant Mark could have more, do more. They never thought of Mark as particularly compliant. It seemed as though his actions—doing well at school, excelling in sports, making friends, attending Hebrew school—were all things he wanted for himself as much as they wanted them for him.

In the middle of eighth grade Mark got pneumonia. When he recovered, he was different, as if a switch had been flipped. He shut them out.

"It's like he's in character," said Miriam, "like he's wearing a costume, a mask. He struts out of his bedroom all puffed up even when it's just me standing there in the hallway with my arms full of laundry, as if I could possibly believe he was tough or rude or mean." After a while she stopped saying that, because at home Mark was tough and rude and mean, which was particularly hard for Miriam to take because with his friends he became more generous and gregarious.

Mark started saying he wasn't a Jew, he was a human being,

an atheist who wasn't going to "undergo" a bar mitzvah. Adam was the one who talked to Miriam. In the end he was the one who said to Mark, "You don't want to be a Jew? Fine, don't be a Jew."

Therese arrived in the doorway of Miriam's room holding two glasses of water. She gave one to Adam.

"I don't think Miriam is breathing," she finally said.

Adam nodded. Miriam was no longer in her body on the bed. Nor was she anywhere Adam could go. He was never going to see his wife again. The utter disorientation he had felt when they lost Mark had been bearable only in that he had shared it with Miriam.

His Miriam. When she was alive it was easy to look past the present grim set of her mouth, back to the pretty petulant pout she put on whenever she had felt like giving him a hard time, which was frequently.

No one else in the world would associate Miriam and mouth and pleasure.

On the other hand, she was released from her pain and he was released from watching her suffer.

He felt the calm after struggle; he felt immense relief.

"Jews don't believe in an afterlife," he told Therese.

"I understand," said Therese, unusually agreeable. Her damp hand squeezed his.

But Miriam was somewhere, watching, he was sure of it.

"Adam?" asked Therese after some time had passed; he couldn't tell how long. "Is there anyone you want me to call?"

"I'll do it later." *I've failed to protect my wife and son.* The thought he was thinking over and over.

"Is it okay if I make a couple calls?"

"Go ahead." Because she left the door open, it was easy to eavesdrop. Miriam would have scolded.

"Jude? Mark's mother just died. Yeah, I'm okay. Yes, I'll tell Adam. You're with Nan? No, I'm fine." Therese let out a sigh. "What?" she asked, sounding suddenly pleased. "You're breaking up with her?"

Adam had never liked Mark's childhood friend Jude. Back when Mark was in middle school, Adam had wanted to spank him for being friends with the kid, because Jude had always struck Adam as low achieving and manipulative. Miriam had told him he couldn't spank Mark for that. It would have been over the line.

As he sat next to Miriam, Adam began thinking about all the times he had spanked Mark. He spanked Mark when Mark bit Miriam. He spanked Mark when he was crying about going to school. He spanked Mark when Mark stole a bag of potato chips from the grocery store. He spanked Mark when Mark wouldn't turn off the television and go to bed. Miriam told him not to spank Mark so much. She knew Mark had begun to remind Adam of his older brother Jeffery, Jeffery who had cut school, smoked cigarettes, chased girls, started drinking at thirteen, and didn't stop until he was dead from liver failure. Mark looked like Adam but his attitude and behavior were like Jeffery's. Adam had never regretted spanking Mark; he regretted not spanking Mark enough.

"Mom?" Therese was making another call. "Yeah, I know it's late." It never took long for Therese to veer toward sharpness with her mother Alice. Alice was another woman who could *talk*.

Adam's strategy as a father had been to say very little because what good would talking have done? Fatherhood was akin to a career with a known trajectory: when the kids are little they adore you; they turn on you as teenagers; they come back when they grow up.

The teenage years had been the worst. In high school Mark cheated on tests. Drank booze from the liquor closet. Adam couldn't spank him when Mark grew bigger than he was and started hitting back.

At that time Adam resorted to cautionary tales featuring his brother Jeffery, with the repeated moral being balance. "You want to go out and be a lunatic, fine, make sure you aren't puking when you come home. Make sure you have a job on the weekend and be there on time. Make sure you do well at school and get into a decent college. Be respectful of your mother. I'm not talking about like, I'm not talking about love, I'm talking about respect. Treat all women with respect. Liking is something else entirely; liking isn't necessary."

During those years Mark and his friends (and of course Miriam too) were all against Reagan. Reagan was a plastic idiot, but he was good for business. They didn't want to see how Reagan's deregulation helped the family grow; they failed to make the connection between the salmon and steak they regularly enjoyed and Ronald Reagan. Mark was still young, and Miriam's sphere at this point was mostly at home. They lived in a world where everyone could share and share alike and there was always enough to go around. Adam lived in the next world over, the world where he was duking it out with men who also wanted the limited supply of steak and salmon.

After high school Mark went to SUNY Binghamton, tuition paid by Adam, and declared his major sociology. He came back that first summer actively criticizing Adam, laughing how Adam had left Brooklyn for Lawnhurst, how he'd left a legitimate city, a vibrant urban center, a real place, to live in its inversion.

Mark told Adam: You think you're climbing the ladder of success but really you're just escaping, you're participating in the same white flight that's crippled all of America's great cities. Definition of banker: *predatory lender*.

Each night that summer Mark helped himself to Adam's Saab to go out with his friends—they liked a club that played the music of their favorite band, The Clash. At home Mark played their albums over and over. His favorite was *Sandinista!*

"Ma." On the phone Therese was growing increasingly irritated. "Is Aleksandar asleep? Good. No, I'll sleep here in Mark's old room. It doesn't feel right to leave Adam alone. Ma, I have to go."

Before Mark went back to school to start his junior year at Binghamton, Adam sat him down and told him he was on his own starting the day after graduation. He was graduating college debt-free and for that he should be grateful. He could not move back home. Adam would not pay his rent. He would not pay for his food. He would neither give him a car, nor would he help pay for a car, or help with payment of car insurance. He would not allow Mark to use his car or Miriam's. He would not pay for Mark's healthcare or health insurance.

Mark changed his major to business and shut his mouth about Reagan.

"I can't believe the nurse isn't back yet." Therese was standing in the doorway, backlit from the light in the kitchen, curls escaping from her rubber band.

"It doesn't matter," said Adam. Months afterward, when he thought of it, however, he found himself fixated and furious because Rose had "missed" Miriam's death. In the moment, however, he had been glad to be alone with his wife.

"What do you want to do?" asked Therese.

After college Mark had gotten a job on Wall Street, and lived in lower Manhattan. He started dating Therese again as he had in high school; she still lived at home with her parents and commuted to college. All Therese's bluster—was it just a cover for a frightened little girl? For a wedding present Adam helped them with a down payment for a house in Lawnhurst.

"Do you want to keep sitting with Miriam?" Therese was asking him gently.

"No." He stood and moved toward her, but she turned and left the room.

He followed her into the kitchen, where they stood looking at each other.

"Are you hungry?" asked Therese. "Can I make you something?"

Adam was aware he'd been relying on his daughter-in-law too much, but there was no one else he wanted to be near. Aleksandar was the most important person in his life, and she was his mother. A baby was on the way. They were his family.

He took a step, reaching for her, and from her expression thought she might run away. Instead she moved into his arms.

It was hard to tell if Therese was clinging to him or if he was clinging to her. His eyes were open. Hers were closed. He put his hand under her chin, kissed her mouth. Her eyes flew open.

Miriam and all her women—the ones she'd known personally, as well as her sisters in spirit—gathered in his mind, a Greek chorus yelling *NO!*

There was the sound of the front door opening. Therese backed away. Adam stared at her while listening to the sounds of Rose stepping inside the house, closing the front door, walking through the foyer and the living room, arriving, finally, in the kitchen.

"I'm so sorry." Rose's gaze swept over Therese where she stood by the sink, and landed on Adam just outside Miriam's room. The harsh overhead light cast shadows under her eyes. "She must be gone." It wasn't a question.

"Yes." Adam looked not at Rose, but at Therese; she was staring at the floor. He had not imagined it. A kiss like that meant something.

And why not, he thought, so much later it was almost dawn. He could not sleep. He'd sat, paced, looked for a moon, but the night was cloudy. The air now at 4:30 a.m. was the coolest it would be in a twenty-four hour period. Birds were beginning to sing. The automatic sprinkler switched on in the yard. He was standing at the threshold of the screened-in porch where he'd set up a cot for Rose, but after Rose facilitated the transport of Miriam's body to the funeral home, she'd gone home. Therese was sleeping on the cot, bare shoulders visible above the white sheet. He wanted to go in, but knew he could not.

Therese would move into his house. She would bring Aleksandar. The baby would arrive, Mark's child, another version of Mark.

Adam was reassured; his epic loss would be replaced by these gifts.

Fidelity

SHORTLY AFTER Miriam died, Therese joined Jude in her backyard after putting Aleksandar to bed. The citronella candles she lit, along with Jude's cigarette, overpowered the scent of the roses Mark had planted along the fence. Jude stood in the far corner of the yard to protect her and the baby from secondhand smoke.

She sat down in a plastic chair and put her bare feet into Aleksandar's half-filled baby pool. Darkness descended. Fireflies blinked on and off.

"You've been assuming the baby is Mark's?" she asked.

"I haven't been assuming anything." Jude took a last drag of his cigarette before putting it out in the ashtray he now kept hidden under the azaleas because he spent most nights here. He crossed the yard and sat down next to her. "But if you have something to tell me, tell me." He began unlacing his sneakers.

"Is it really over between Nan and you?"

"There wasn't much to end." Jude pulled off his socks.

Therese had met Nan once. She was taller than Jude, her long straight brown hair accentuating angularity: cheekbones, jawbone, collar bones. She was a rich girl from Rhode Island and looked it, despite her checkered pants and clogs, her

Brooklynesque tattoos. She'd smiled warmly at Therese, making it abundantly clear she knew all about her and felt confidently superior. Therese was sure Nan didn't have trouble letting go when Jude ended it.

Therese was having trouble acknowledging she and Jude were truly alone together; there was no one else. She wasn't used to it yet. She was used to sneaking around and wryly evading. Used to being a creep. It had never felt ethically right, but it had been her pattern. It had been familiar.

Everything shifted after Mark died. It was as if the world clicked into the nearby space it always should have occupied. Therese knew she should be grieving and she was, some of the time. But as she began spending more time with Jude, life began to feel far less dispiriting than it had when Mark was alive.

It wasn't just Mark's absence and Jude's presence. It was Jude's presence along with the presence of Aleksandar and the baby. She kept thinking the two of them were like yeast. This growth, or beauty, or joy she felt, she didn't know what to call it, was tenuous, untested.

She put her hand on her belly. Was she feeling movement? Maybe she was just hungry.

"Kevin is the baby's father." There was no other way to say it.

"Are you shitting me?" Jude rested his feet on the lip of the pool instead of submerging them.

"I was with him the night Mark died."

"You're insane."

"I know."

Jude pulled his cigarettes from his pocket and tumbled the pack in his hands.

"I've been afraid to tell you," Therese continued. She felt herself suddenly on the verge of hysteria. Jude was right.

Adopting a child with Mark had been insane. Having sex with Kevin had been insane. Having Kevin's baby was insane.

"I'm taking a walk." Jude grabbed his sneakers. He skirted the side of the house instead of walking through it.

Therese felt a kick. Definitely a kick.

A Day at the Beach

PAUL HUMMED along with the radio as he drove. The Oldsmobile had not been full for years. The people in it as well as the world beyond it, the streets and sidewalks, the spindly trees and squat buildings, felt pleasingly remote.

Salt water is good for cuts, thought Alice in the passenger seat. Something her mother had said. Her short slim mother had rolled clean socks and placed them in Alice's top dresser drawer. She'd found many reasons to hit Alice; the nuns had too.

Ridiculous top forty song lyrics floated above the air conditioning. Adam suffered in the back seat. Only his grandson, adjacent, assuaged him. Adam didn't trust Alice or Paul with Aleksandar. Their parenting track record was questionable, but so was his.

Aleksandar stared out the window. The stuffed dog on his lap was as tan and limp as the good one, but it didn't smell right. The good one might be squished between his bedroom wall and bed, might be under the bed, might be in bed under a blanket.

Alice had tried to keep the supplies minimal. Still, they needed to eat.

Paul lugged the watery iced tea, blanket, and two aluminum chairs, Adam the umbrella and tote full of towels, Alice, a thermos of coffee and cooler with tuna in pitas and a bag of red grapes. Aleksandar gripped a plastic shovel and pail. The dog he'd left in the car, mashed into the door's cup holder.

Upon reaching the boardwalk, the grandparents stripped down to bathing suits, to loose spotty skin. Alice pulled Aleksandar's t-shirt over his head, daubed lotion onto his chest and back, slathered his legs, tilted his chin, dotted his face, rubbed it all in.

"Take off your shoes," said Grandpa Paul.

Aleksandar shook his head.

"Has he been to the beach before?" asked Alice, shocked not to know this essential fact about her only grandson. Be fair, she told herself, you've only known him six months. He'd spent his first four years in a Bulgarian orphanage. She pointed at the sand. "It's easier to walk without shoes."

Down the ramp and toward the ocean Aleksandar marched. Sturdy, stiff, resolute. Was he even three feet tall? Alice hurried to keep up.

It was too early for lifeguards. Seagulls cried as they cut the air. Fishermen close to the jetties wore jeans, old sneakers, hooded sweatshirts, the buttS of their long fishing rods jammed into wet sand. Low tide.

Paul settled the blanket, unfolded the chairs. Adam opened the umbrella. Aleksandar dropped his shovel and pail. Alice knew they would have to keep watch, and when the tide began to come in, move back. Where the water receded, plastic and dead things remained: tampon inserters, half eaten crabs.

Alice recalled a huge black sculpture she and Paul had seen

not long ago in a museum in the city. It was contained in a specially built room, viewable only through oddly shaped and located windows, some close to the floor, some high and hard to reach. Impossible to view in its entirety.

"Aleksandar," directed Alice. "Put your bare tootsies in the ocean. Ah," she moaned, illustrating, the water rising above her ankles.

Aleksandar sat down on wet sand and removed his sandals. Feeling trapped was familiar. Wide-open spaces were confusingly exhilarating. He ran as fast as he could through the clear shallow water, climbed onto the rock jetty, and was chased off by his grandmother. He ran up dry sand, Pop Pop behind him, the sand warmer and warmer under his feet until it was cold.

"Get out of there." Adam, crouching, yanked Aleksandar back into sunshine. "People used to do heroin under the boardwalk. There might still be a needle, deep in the sand." He reflexively thought of his son Mark, and the drugs he'd enjoyed until they killed him. On the way back to the blanket, he paused to delineate acceptable parameters. "The garbage can by the boardwalk is too far." Aleksandar could go as far as the lifeguard stand, where a sleepy-looking young man and woman now climbed to their bench. Adam could no longer envision the solid thing he'd spent his life climbing towards; whatever it had been had become a trick of light, of shadow.

Back at the blanket, Grandpa Paul held a large white clamshell.

"Let's try something," he said.

"First hydrate." Grandma Alice pushed paper cups. Everyone dutifully drank.

"Aleksandar, come over here." Grandpa Paul had dug a

shallow trench. "Lie down on your back and close your eyes," he said. "I'm going to bury you."

Aleksandar lay down in the trench.

Grandpa Paul pushed wet sand against the sides of Aleksandar's hips, and carefully across his pelvis, and down over his legs and feet. Pop Pop dumped buckets of wet sand until Aleksandar's thin chest disappeared and he felt sand at his neck threatening his face; he loved to be touched; he hated to be touched; he felt like weeping when anyone touched him; he could not allow himself to weep.

Alice looked at the waves. She hated games most especially burying, poking, tickling, hide and seek.

"He'll never break free!" Grandpa Paul used his best evil dictator voice.

"He can't move his fingers or his toes," Pop Pop intoned.

"Is he really stuck?" Alice tried not to shriek.

Aleksandar continued moving his fingers, as he'd been doing the entire time his grandfathers were burying him.

Pop Pop: "He's a goner for sure."

Grandpa Paul: "Dead as a doornail."

Aleksandar shifted his arms and legs. The sand fell away.

"Argh!" yelled both grandfathers.

Aleksandar sat up, lifting arms and legs one by one.

"Don't let him escape!" yelled Grandpa Paul.

Aleksandar stomped around the blanket, pumped his fist in the air. A trace of sand clung to his spine. "Again," he said, returning to the trench.

"For Pete's sake!" Sweat rolled down between Alice's breasts, down her torso, pooled into her squashed navel. Aleksandar had been buried multiple times. "Let's swim!"

Adam watched Aleksandar walk into the water between

Alice and Paul. He would remain vigilant from shore. In Brooklyn, growing up, he never learned to swim.

Aleksandar twisted and yelled, as the waves rolled against him, higher and higher.

"Look at the other kids," instructed Grandpa Paul. "Jump like them."

Aleksandar tried to do what the other kids were doing.

It hurt Paul and Alice's shoulders to be jerked; they'd reverted to parent mode, ignoring the pain. The ocean rose above their thighs. They knelt down and lifted their hands, still gripping Aleksandar's.

The tide was coming in, the briny smell, so strong at low tide, now an undertone, more memory than odor. As a child Alice dove under the water and opened her eyes while she swam, holding her breath, hoping to see something, but the light from the sky only filtered so far, the water beyond that murky, unknowable.

Aleksandar's eyes wide, mouth salty. The ocean slapped and licked.

"Salt water helps you float," announced Grandpa Paul.

"Let go of Grandpa, Aleksandar, and put your hands on my shoulders." Still kneeling, Grandma Alice turned her body perpendicular to the shore. "Good. Now jump a little bit. See if you can stretch out on your belly and kick your feet."

Aleksandar faced her, held onto her shoulders. Beyond that he had no idea what she was trying to get him to do.

"I can't stay balanced," she said. The waves were minor, but the current still pulled. "This isn't going to work."

"Look at those kids," directed Grandpa Paul. Some were on top of the water with their bodies, some were on foam boards, traveling swiftly toward sand. "Now we're going to do it," he muttered. He maneuvered Aleksandar's body until he was facing the shore. "Squat like me." He demonstrated and reached for Aleksandar's hand. He pushed off, into the water, pulling Aleksandar alongside. "Move your arms!" he yelled. "Kick your feet!"

Waves pushed at Alice's back. "Ride it out!"

Aleksandar felt liberating momentum, further saltiness, the exhilarating freedom of the present, free from regret or anticipation, the ocean rushing back toward the beach where Pop Pop stood clapping. Aleksandar jumped up, took Grandpa Paul's hand, helped him struggle to his feet, pulled him toward the waves, staggered back in.

Lunch time. A ritual from their daughters' childhoods: Paul held Aleksandar's hands, instructing the child to plop his butt down on the blanket. Alice placed a clean towel across his lap. Paul handed him his tuna pita.

Adam lowered himself, groaning, to sit next to Aleksandar.

Aleksandar dropped a hunk of his pita into the sand and looked around to see what would happen.

"Darn it," said Adam, reaching over and tossing the pita. A gull swooped down and hopped off with it.

Aleksandar watched, eyes wide, as other gulls swooped and swarmed.

Alice unscrewed the thermos, poured a cup, took a sip. "This coffee," she said, "is as good as the coffee in Rome."

"I'm glad you're happy," said Paul.

"Who said I was happy?" said Alice. Death was so close, so recent, and Adam right here.

Paul got up from his chair to lay face down on the blanket.

Adam kept his eyes trained on the ocean. He had not enjoyed his own marital squabbles. Did these two imagine he enjoyed theirs?

Alice had forgotten how lucky she was to live near the ocean. It had been years since she'd been to the beach! She watched Aleksandar dig with his hands. His plastic shovel had broken almost immediately. His hole began to fill with water. He yelled in surprise. Was he lonely without a playmate? When Alice was a girl, there had always been plenty of kids: brothers, sisters, cousins, neighbors. Children had been as common as starlings.

Adam's mirrored sunglasses masked his eyes. Alice knew from experience he would refuse any comfort offered. She and Paul had gone to his house to sit Shiva after his wife Miriam died, a few months after Mark. Alice made and brought a pound cake, for which she was thanked before it was removed to the kitchen, never to be seen again. Shiva turned out to be Adam and his neighbors, extended relatives, and friends, sitting in the living room. Alice looked for mirrors draped with cloth. She'd read about that custom, as well as sitting on old crates. She didn't see any mirrors, covered or otherwise. People sat on regular living room furniture. They took turns reminiscing about Miriam: she'd loved Mahjong, estate sales, painting, and most of all, her son Mark. At one moment everyone fell silent, and stared at Miriam's floral acrylics on the walls. Alice was sure she could smell vanilla from the pound cake drifting into the living room. There had been no Shiva for Mark. Therese had insisted upon a wake, though she was far more lapsed than Catholic. Alice admitted ambivalence about her daughter's habitual disregard for other people. If Therese was unkind, she was also brave; she made other people seem tame. Though it was Miriam's Shiva, Alice found herself mourning her son-in-law. To refocus, she conjured Miriam's grim face and puffed white hair, her impeccable blouses and slacks.

Alice wedged her cup into the sand so the coffee wouldn't spill. She was resolved to apologize for Therese's infidelity, though Paul always insisted Mark was an addict long before he married Therese.

"Sleeping with other men does not improve one's marriage," Alice had always said in response, but here the conversation stopped, for Paul did not want to talk about his daughter's sex life, and for once Alice felt the same way he did.

On the blanket, Aleksandar pretended to sleep until he fell asleep.

Paul draped him with towels and repositioned the umbrella to protect him from the sun. He found his book in the towel bag and sat down in one of the chairs to read.

"I'm going to stretch my legs," said Alice. "Do either of you want to join me?"

"I'll watch Aleksandar." Paul preferred modernist classics.

Alice made a face. She enjoyed the tumult of high fantasy, knights and ladies, swords and sorcerers, codes of chivalry, mystical earth religions, barbarians, sex, violence, and truth-telling dwarves.

"I'll walk." Adam's ancient social training meant he was unable to refuse an invitation from a woman.

Alice pushed aside her suit straps and rubbed an additional layer of sunscreen onto her shoulders, imagining for a moment what the years would have been like, how they would have been different, had she been married to Adam.

Adam stood and waited while Alice got herself together: sunscreen, long shirt, floppy hat. The way she paid attention to herself now made Adam certain she had been pretty in her youth. Miriam would not have liked Alice's tiger-striped bathing suit or gauzy mauve cover-up.

Alice had to run to keep up with his stride. A blue t-shirt hung from his stooped shoulders. She tried to decide whether his anguished face prevented actual handsomeness, or made him handsome. Adam suspected all women wanted something unnamable from men, something intangible no man could hope to either identify or provide. It hurt him still, Miriam's unflagging belief in his inadequacy.

"I hope Therese is having a good first day back," said Alice. She and Paul and Adam would be taking care of Aleksandar for the summer. They would be rotating weeks. Today, Therese's first day back at work, Alice had wanted them all to be together. "I'm excited about the baby, of course," said Alice, "though I'm not sure how it's all going to work. I'm just trying not to worry too much, but it's hard."

Adam knew he was supposed to say Therese would be fine, everything would be fine.

"Miriam always thought Therese would do something drastic," he said. "And then when it happened, it was Mark." He was embarrassed to notice, as they walked, how long his toenails had grown, how much they needed clipping.

"Did you ever think that instead of worrying about keeping our children alive, we'd worry they didn't want to live?"

Adam emitted a strangled laugh.

"When they were teenagers. That's when that started," said Alice.

They walked on in silence. Alice watched women as they jogged past, the confident ones in bikinis, the others in shorts.

"Therese can be a difficult girl for us to love." According to Paul, saying "us" and "we" when she really meant "me" was one of her horrible flaws. His was a complete lack of humor. "When Therese was growing up, we fought about everything." Alice refrained from telling Adam when this dynamic had changed. When Therese married Mark, her fury had found a new target. "Therese cheated on Mark." She paused for a millisecond. "I'm so sorry."

Adam knew it was his turn to speak. The Catholic wanted her absolution. She didn't understand how little he now had, how he could no longer afford to be generous. All he had was the magma of his grief. All he could do was protect it.

As the silence stretched, the minutes passed, Alice felt the descent of motherly dread replacing her grandmotherly enthusiasm. The days of summer stretched out endlessly in front of her, as they did when her daughters were children. What would they do with Aleksandar all summer? What would Adam do during his weeks of caretaking? The man's child had been a drug addict; she could not help searching for a reason. Mark had left a wife and child—a recently adopted child—as well as a soon-to-be-born baby. What about Adam? She wanted an apology from him!

"Let's head back." Alice spun in the sand. "School will help," she said, as if he asked to be reassured. "In September, Aleksandar starts kindergarten."

They walked back toward the blanket.

Adam knew Alice wasn't finished with him. She would continue to seek him out. She would work on him and work on him. He knew her desire. It was boundless, limitless, without end. She has told herself she simply wants closure, but he knew in fact she wanted a relationship.

"It's only June," he finally said.

"Late June," she corrected. Soon it would be July. In August, jellyfish would wash up on the beach, poisonous red threads visible. September shimmered like a mirage. Despite her own experience, Alice believed school would provide safety and security for Aleksandar. The rectangular solidity of the building, the number of responsible people involved, teachers, lunch ladies, the principal. She thought of these nonfamily members as unbiased observers, individuals from a neutral country monitoring a fraught election.

The blanket came into view: Paul still reading, Aleksandar sleeping. People used words like regret or guilt or sorrow. Adam could distill them all into one word: dislocation. He was banished from himself. Only in the presence of Aleksandar did he feel at home.

Alice took a lengthy, solo swim.

Aleksandar woke up and built a complicated castle with Pop Pop.

Paul continued to read until a creeping distraction—vodka tonics and salted peanuts—settled in.

Alice emerged from the ocean wrinkled, dripping.

Paul looked up from his book. "What do you say we get a move on?"

"Good," said Alice. "Beat the traffic. Adam, are you ready?

"It's time to go, son." Adam threw his clam shell into the hole.

"No." Aleksandar continued to dig.

"Aleksandar, it's time," said Grandpa Paul.

Aleksandar jumped up and threw himself onto the sandy blanket. He sobbed and kicked his feet.

Paul looked at Alice and Adam. They shrugged at one another, and began to pack the chairs, cooler, umbrella, towels.

Aleksandar grew tired of crying. He breathed into the space between his mouth and the blanket. The air tasted like heat. He still needed to dig. What would become of their castle? The kids nearby would play with it, destroy it, but first act like they had built it. It had been the same at the orphanage: adults always deciding what would happen next. Aleksandar rolled onto his back and drew a quivering breath of resignation.

"Lordy," said Alice. "I forgot about leaving the beach."

"Aleksandar, put on your sandals. The sand near the boardwalk is hot. When we get there, we'll get ice cream."

Alice smiled at Paul. Pure genius! Remembering the power of a bribe.

It was slow going for the elderly in flip-flops. Aleksandar, running, reached the boardwalk first. The booth sold Italian ices. Aleksandar wanted rainbow; Alice requested lemon. So did Paul. On an empty bench they all sat down. Red and blue juice dribbled from Aleksandar's chin.

"I'm praying for us all." Alice knew both men would be irritated by her religiosity and the quaver in her voice. She prayed while she walked, while she cooked, while she cleaned, while she read, while she slept, though she knew God wasn't taking any orders disguised as prayers, at least not from her. Adam focused on his cherry ice, on perfecting a balance of melt and solidity. Aleksandar remembered the dog in the car. Now that he had been punished, he might be okay. Paul pointed to a prop plane pulling an advertisement for chewing gum. They all looked up, watched it disappear behind a cloud.

Fix It? Or Run?

HURRICANE IRENE landed at the end of August. By sunrise the worst was over. Kevin checked out the beach. A two-story lifeguard station had been swept up the sand. It was jammed sideways against the boardwalk. He didn't have time to walk around and investigate further. He'd already ranked the frantic messages on his voice mail.

An image of Therese rose up as Kevin drove, the mingled odors of seawater and sewage flowing through his van's rolled-down windows. She'd been showing up in his dreams, as she had back in high school.

In these dreams Therese seemed to embody, rather than the promise of pleasure, fulfillment. Each dream ended with her slipping from his grasp. Waking, he forced himself to shake off the feeling the dream evoked—that of being loved.

Therese is a dead end, he reminded himself. You've been down enough of those already.

The streets of Long Beach were flooded at the corners where drains were backed up. The water wouldn't recede until low tide.

At his first job of the day, behind a screen door stood a man exactly Kevin's height. Old enough to be my father, thought

Kevin, though many men were. Why think that particular thought while looking at this poor slob, his stained T-shirt straining across his belly?

"Here's the plumber." The guy's eyes zeroed in on Kevin's. He pushed the screen door open, and Kevin stepped inside, the house immediately narrowing, the living room furniture covered in books and magazines, the view of the hall obscured by piles of newspapers. Filled plastic bags sat on top of the piles. He tried not to imagine what might be inside them. A multi-sourced odor filled the house: undone laundry, dirty dishes left too long, a rarely scrubbed bathroom. Some people got to live with people they loved, windows open, succulent houseplants on windowsills, fruit and flowers in bowls. The ones that got to Kevin were the ones who lived alone, their gummy kitchen counters lined with cans.

"This way."

The trail down the hallway made Kevin think first of a deer path, and then, as the piles of newspapers on either side of the hall began to rise, a crevasse. His former fiancée Michele, homesick for Oregon, had a thing for words describing landscapes. Whenever she'd come across one in a newspaper or a magazine she'd read it out loud: *butte*, *ravine*, *gully*, *mudflat*, *riprap*.

"Won't flush." The man pointed at the toilet, turning to squeeze his belly past Kevin to walk down the hallway, disappearing the way people did when their shit was floating in the bowl, when there was nothing they could do to make it go away.

After unplugging the toilet and draining three nearby basements, it was time for a break, the strip club Kevin's habitual mid-morning pit stop.

Clean bathrooms, cool air, hot girls, large Cokes.

The post-club smoke in his van in the parking lot was also routine, though the pipe was new; he'd ordered it online. It was glass, heavier than his old acrylic one had been, and a mix of swirling colors. The old one had been black. He'd kept track of it for so long; he couldn't figure out where he'd misplaced it.

If he thought about it, it bothered him, the girls in the club getting comparatively younger and younger, the layers of emotion—feigned enthusiasm, fear, fatigue—they wore as vividly as eye shadow. He could remember a time when all he saw was sumptuous flesh, when his response was rigidly automatic.

Now he witnessed their pity—he was getting a little old—and pitied them right back. Stripping wasn't a trade, there were no unions, no benefits for girls in their platform shoes at their poles. At least they had a job. The unemployment rate in New York was still at 9.1%, and would be, according to the news, until at least 2012.

Just before leaving the parking lot, Kevin answered his ringing phone. It was Jude.

"You working?" Jude of course made no mention of the hurricane. Self-absorbed since fourth grade when they'd met, he'd only gotten worse as he grew up and became a Manhattanite.

"Yeah, I'm working." Kevin made more money as a plumber than Jude did as a copywriter, but Jude still acted superior. Mark had been the uncontested rich man of their trio.

"I'm on my way out to the Island," said Jude. "Come meet me?"

Make a clean break, Kevin told himself. You've been relegated to the kind of old friend to be called whenever

Jude deigns to come home. He never invites you into the city to have dinner or go to a concert or meet his other friends. He wants to keep you in your box, keep being the winner to your loser. Now that Mark's gone there's no reason to pretend you're all still friends.

"Be at Finnegan's in twenty." Was Jude informing or commanding?

Kevin heard himself say okay. He'd have one drink, and then get back to work.

The bar was located near the massive grey trestle of the Long Island Rail Road. Without mountains or hills, the trestle was the south shore's defining landmark. It was also a reminder, a rebuke. They were an extremity. Without blood from the city, they would wither.

When Kevin's eyes adjusted to the dark interior he saw a lone woman sitting at the far corner table. She stood up; she was wearing a loose sundress. She held out her arms.

He hadn't seen Therese since Mark's wake, when he'd broken down sobbing in front of the priest; Therese had walked past several times, ignoring him. She'd called him a couple times since then, most recently the night her mother-in-law died. She wasn't calling to get together with him that was clear. It was as if she had called to talk to him about something important, but instead made pointless chitchat, and he put up with it, because number one he worried about her and number two from her he would put up with anything.

"I'll have a Corona and the fried shrimp," Kevin told the ancient man behind the bar as he walked toward Therese.

Back in high school he'd forbidden himself to be attracted to her, though he could never control his dreams. High-strung, high-maintenance beauties were not for men like him. His girls, like Michele, were sturdy, self-sufficient, pretty.

When Therese had called out of the blue in the spring asking him to come over to "help with a project" he had been flattered and then triumphant.

He realized Mark was home in the basement only after his stroke.

"I didn't know you'd be here." Kevin reflexively hugged Therese. She felt both round and firm. Probably drowning her sorrow in ice cream. Curves accentuated her beauty, but all of life seemed to, even the sad parts. Neither the brand nor the quantity of her perfume had changed since high school, so strong he could taste it.

She gripped his hands, stepped back to study him.

"You look good."

Kevin knew his greasy coveralls suited him. When he looked in the mirror after his evening shower, the man in the clean T-shirt appeared unfamiliar. Only his hands looked consistent, strong, and never entirely clean.

You're not a bad man, Kevin told himself. You're neither a heroin addict nor a self-absorbed asshole.

"How was the hurricane in Lawnhurst?" he asked. "You didn't lose power, did you?"

"Nothing big happened. Wind. A ton of rain. Is Long Beach insane?"

"Flooding and assorted bullshit." As was the case whenever Kevin saw Therese, he found it difficult to fix her in the present, like him, almost forty years old. The popular, powerful girl she'd been in high school emanated from her like a hologram.

But she was no longer a skinny high school girl who starved herself; her hair now dyed its rich red-brown.

"How are you doing?" he asked, though he clearly felt the aura of both life and death in the air around him.

"Let's sit," she said finally, letting go of his hands.

"How's your little boy?"

The boy had been home that day, too, asleep or at least pretending. Kevin didn't often allow himself to think about it—what he'd done with Therese while her husband and son *were in the house*—it didn't matter that Kevin hadn't known they were there.

After they found Mark, Therese pushed Kevin out the back door while the boy hung onto her leg.

"Go! Go!" She screamed until he'd finally left.

"Aleksandar's confused, I think," she said now. A whiskey, neat, sat on the table in front of her, and next to that a tall glass of water.

"How are you?" she asked.

Guilt-ridden and lonely, he wanted to tell her. I love it that you called me. I want you to call me all the time.

"I'm good," he said. "Busy as hell."

"The rest of us are like spinning tops banging into each other, flying off. You're steady, Kevin. It's taken me too long to appreciate that quality."

Kevin knew it was wrong to confirm his dependability; he'd lived long enough to not trust what women said they liked about men. She liked stability? Bullshit. Yet he felt her heat from across the table, and wondered if it could mean something.

It had happened once, it could happen again, he encouraged himself. He considered placing a hand on her knee.

"Here's Jude," said Therese, looking over at the door.

Jude and the barkeep arrived at the table together.

Kevin had completely forgotten about Jude's phone call, and here he was, grown fat in the months since the night with Kathleen. Middle age descending! Jude stood waiting for the elaborate handshake, the half-lean-half-hug, until Kevin obliged wondering how he could work his weight—same as in high school—into the conversation.

"Did you tell him?" Jude asked Therese. "We're getting married."

"You got fat," said Kevin.

Jude ignored this, leaning to kiss and smooth Therese's hair before sitting next to her, the two of them facing him across the table.

The bartender placed the Corona on the table, backed away.

"Remember when I was seeing your sister Joanna?" asked Kevin.

Neither Therese nor Jude responded. Jude took a sip of his drink and put his arm around Therese's shoulders.

Kevin took a long slug of beer.

"Remember, Therese?" he persisted. "Remember when you and Mark, and me and Joanna went on a double date? Mark borrowed his father's car, and we all went to play miniature golf?"

"Your thing with Joanna didn't last very long." Therese's eyes narrowed competitively.

"No. Remember she told you I was 'too Long Island,' and dumped me?" Kevin watched Therese and Jude smile wryly.

Being "too Long Island" or "totally Long Island" was something people had said back in high school to indicate a person's lack of sophistication, their limitation of scope. Kevin could sense that for Therese and Jude, as for himself, the residue of having been judged remained.

"I was there that night, too," said Jude. "You don't remember? I beat you all at mini-golf. And then I hit a hole-in-one at the end, and won a free game."

"Therese, remember Michele?" It felt urgent, suddenly, for Kevin to say her name.

"Michele, yuck." Therese employed the old finger down the throat gesture.

The smell of frying shrimp filled the air. The tiny kitchens in these places consisted of a vat of hot oil behind the bar.

The image of Michele Kevin enjoyed most was her exulting in the sun in her bikini on Long Beach.

They had been together two years. Kevin had even visited her family in Portland. According to her, the Oregon coast was "close," but it had taken two hours to drive there, past office parks, and new housing developments, and farms, and finally through a forest, the Pacific Ocean surprising him on the other side.

Gigantic rocks jutted up in the surf. Though it had been summer, the only people who went near the ocean were children. They were like shore birds—darting, running, crying, pecking at the sand.

"Earth to Kevin." Therese waved a hand in front of his face. "Why are we talking about you getting stood up at the altar? Did you hear what Jude said? We're getting married! You're the first to know."

"There was no altar," said Kevin. "We were at the City Clerk's office on Worth Street."

"Dude, let it go," muttered Jude.

"God, it was awful," said Therese, finally warming, as Kevin had hoped, to the seductive momentum of nostalgia. "Remember how Mark kept insisting Michele was just running late? He wanted to call the restaurant and move the reservation back an hour. He and I were to be witnesses," she explained, though over the years Jude had probably heard each detail of the story a dozen times. "We were going to host the celebratory lunch at this restaurant near the Stock Exchange, a steak place Mark loved. Mark was Kevin's best man." Therese smiled wistfully. "Remember that girl who finally called you, Kevin? Michele's friend? What was her name?"

"Pamela," Jude said flatly.

"Wipe that smirk off your face," said Kevin.

"Nobody's smirking!" said Therese.

Kevin had spoken to Pamela on the phone. "Is Michele sick?"

"Michele isn't sick." Pamela sounded both terrified and thrilled. "Michele doesn't want to get married."

"What did you say?" Kevin walked a few paces from where he'd been standing next to Mark; Therese had followed him. "Can you speak up?" The hallway was swarming with brides and grooms.

"She doesn't want to marry you!" yelled Pamela. "She totally apologizes, but she changed her mind!"

"Give me the phone," Therese had had to demand several times before Kevin complied.

"Tell *Michele* we always hated her. Tell *Michele* her clothes are cheap, her hair is lame, and even if she could lose that last ten pounds she would still look like shit. Thank *Michele* for sparing Kevin a lifetime of boredom, lame sex, and overall misery. I have to get off the phone now. We're going to eat lobster and drink champagne."

When Therese handed the phone back to Kevin it felt slick with lotion and sweat.

For several moments Kevin couldn't move. He couldn't even think his almost-wife's name—Therese had slaughtered it.

It was Mark who had taken his elbow and walked him out of the City Clerk's office. Kevin had no memory of getting to the wood-paneled restaurant, only of collapsing into a velvet booth, putting his head down on the mahogany table.

The bartender set down the basket of fried shrimp, and pulled the ketchup away from the wall to make sure Kevin saw it.

"How many months has it been since Mark died?" Kevin squeezed an obscene amount of ketchup onto his fried shrimp. "Can't you two just keep fucking each other?"

"Shut up, Kevin." Young/old Therese glared out from eleventh grade, haughty and superior. "We wanted you to be the first to know about the wedding."

"You know it won't work."

"Because you're the marriage expert, right?"

Big surprise, Therese trying to hurt him while Jude sat there like a king waiting for his subject to accept his fate.

"We all knew about your bullshit affair," said Kevin. "Including Mark."

"Kevin," warned Therese.

"Kevin what?" He could open his mouth right now and tell Jude that he too had had sex with Therese.

"Kevin, please." She knew it too. He could shit all over their little fantasy.

"Getting married is good." Therese grabbed a napkin to clean a drop of water on the table, as if she could become instantly prim.

Kevin's phone rang. He had to get back to work. He had to get the hell out of here. But it was his mother's number. His mother never called; Aunt Helen did the calling.

"Mom, what's up? Everything okay?"

"Your Aunt fell off the ladder. I think her ankle is broken. She said she isn't feeling very well."

"Mom, call 911."

"It's nothing like that, I'm sure."

"Call 911."

"No," said his mother. "Helen doesn't like that kind of fuss. I'm sure we'll be fine." Her voice trailed off.

"I'll be there in a few." Kevin watched Jude pay the bar tab.

"Okay then." His mother ended the call.

"Jude and I will follow you to your house." Therese extracted her keys from her bag.

"I don't need your help."

"Fuck you, Kevin. We're your friends. Let's go."

Kevin's mother and Aunt Helen had a predictable schedule, a circumscribed range. Like most New Yorkers, work was paramount in their lives. They spent Monday through Saturday in their shop on Northern Boulevard in Queens, making floral arrangements for weddings, anniversaries, funerals, quinceañeras, bar and bat mitzvahs. Only Sundays were variable. If they craved nature, they took a ten-minute drive in Aunt Helen's wood-paneled station wagon to Hempstead Lake State Park, walked the paved trail through a stand of oaks. For culture they took the train into the city to attend the ballet. His mother believed Lincoln Center the height of elegance, her patent leather shoes reflecting the shining glass, white buildings, outdoor fountain, and enormous chandeliers.

Kevin parked his van in front of the house where he'd lived from the time he was ten until he moved out at eighteen. Therese and Jude followed him up the walk.

"Hello," he called as he opened the door.

"Kevin." Athletic Aunt Helen lay on the couch. She lifted her cheek for his kiss. "Oh good, you've brought company."

Countless times he'd come home to find not Aunt Helen but his mother reclining, the filmy living room sheers drawn across the front windows, various pages of the newspaper folded and scattered on the carpet, his mother's glass and ashtray on the coffee table, the room gently gray with smoke, a fan in the corner, oscillating.

"Lovely to see you, Therese and Jude," said Aunt Helen. "Though I'm a bit of a mess today. Therese, I'm so sorry for your loss."

"Thank you." Therese knelt down next to the couch. "May I see your ankle?"

Kevin's mother came through the swinging door from the kitchen, cigarette tilting from the corner of her mouth. She lit it with a match.

"Hello, my dears," she said, shaking her hand to extinguish the flame. Her Irish accent was practically undimmed. "Jude, I haven't seen you in forever, though just last week I saw your lovely mother at the library."

"Hello Mrs. Maloney." Jude stood near the door, looking as uncomfortable with parents now as he'd been as a teenager.

"Therese, I see your dad sometimes in the supermarket, too." She smiled ruefully. "We are all getting old. But you are glowing." Kevin saw it was true; despite the aftermath of death, Therese did look happier.

"Helen's ankle is really swollen," said Therese. "We should ice it."

"I just now managed to get her inside," said Kevin's mother.

"We limped in together," said Aunt Helen.

"Jude, can you get some ice?" asked Therese.

Jude disappeared through the swinging door.

"Kevin, how is it out there?" asked his mother. "Are you getting a million calls because of the hurricane? We listened to the radio earlier, and watched the news." His mother made no move to touch him.

For as long as he could remember, she kept herself distant beneath floating cigarette smoke and event-specific fabrics: tailored cotton or wool for the flower shop, stiff velvet and satin for the ballet. Today in jeans and a T-shirt, her graying, usually-unmoored hair clamped down with bobby pins, she looked like a different person. When he visited on Sundays to mow the grass, change light bulbs, or trim the hedges, his mother usually lay on the couch while Aunt Helen attended to a variety of never-ending tasks: watering house plants, sewing loose buttons, clipping coupons, changing the records on the turntable she'd owned since her teens, the records, too, from that era: Nat King Cole, Ray Charles, Elvis Presley, Patsy Cline, all the while intermittently returning to the bottle of sherry on the coffee table to replenish his mother's glass; on Sundays his mother was never quite drunk or quite sober.

"Is Long Beach entirely flooded?" His mother employed the girlish smile that worked so well on him and on Aunt Helen.

"A mess," said Kevin.

"The power went out at our shop!" exclaimed his mother. "We've been assured that by tomorrow everything should be back to normal, only it won't be, will it, with Helen laid up." She was trying not to sound petulant.

"I'm sure I'll be fine," said Aunt Helen.

The sound of Jude cracking ice from trays in the kitchen made its way into the living room. Kevin held out his hand and his mother passed the cigarettes and matches. Poor Aunt Helen, her shining shins exposed. He could not recall the exact moment when he understood she was his mother's lover. He'd been three when he and his mother left Cork. He remembered neither Ireland, nor the move to Queens. His earliest memories were of the storefront bakeries his mother called "Spanish" where she bought him rolls crusted with pink sugar. His first memory of Aunt Helen collided with her car; it was necessary in summer to bring along a towel in order to sit on the blistering vinyl seats.

When he was ten, his mother informed him they were moving to Long Island, to Lawnhurst. Aunt Helen drove, and Kevin, in the back seat, awaited a bridge or tunnel. The station wagon contained all they owned: his bike, a few boxes of clothes, one of dishes, his aunt's stereo, her stack of records. It took twenty minutes that Sunday morning to drive from Queens to Lawnhurst, into the driveway of this very house. A few rotting jack-o-lanterns sat on the steps of the house next door. One lone kid threw a baseball into the air, running beneath it with his mitt. Later that day he met the kid: Mark. Jude's family had lived around the block; his mother lived there still.

"How is this place an island?" Kevin had asked his mother. He'd been planning to bike its perimeter.

"Here you go." Jude, back from the kitchen, handed Therese a plastic bag full of ice. The marriage would make Jude Aleksandar's father. The kid was too young to remember Mark very long. Another sweet example of life's big fuck you.

"It's too cold to put the ice directly on her skin," said Therese. "We need a dishtowel."

"Mom," said Kevin, since his mother hadn't moved. "Is there a dishtowel we can use?"

"In the kitchen," said Aunt Helen, "in the—"

"We've got it," said Kevin. "Mom lives here, too. Come on, Mom."

In the kitchen, his mother opened drawer after drawer.

"Why don't you know where things are?" he accused.

"I know where things are!" His mother placed her cigarette in the ashtray on the counter with the air of a queen resting her scepter.

"Did you find a towel?" called Therese from the living room.

His mother turned to open another drawer and triumphantly turned back, brandishing a towel. Kevin had always felt her attachment to him was neither deep nor strong; it felt in no way irrational, no way passionate. She cared for him dutifully, like a pet she had not requested.

In high school he'd asked about his father.

His mother insisted there was nothing to tell.

"Your father evaporated in Ireland."

"What do you mean *evaporated*?"

"Must I spell it out? It was a one-night fling."

"Why even *have* the baby then?"

"You couldn't get an abortion in Ireland," she'd quietly said.

Kevin regretted the way he'd stood there, feeling everything, saying nothing.

His mother had never admitted she'd ruined his life by not loving him.

"Why do you think I haven't married?" he asked her now.

"Kevin." The smoke from his mother's cigarette in the ashtray rose in a single curving line. One of the bobby pins in her hair was about to slip out. "How am I supposed to know something like that?" The stress of Aunt Helen's injury showed on her face. "I suppose you've picked women who don't want to marry you."

"Why was Aunt Helen on a ladder? What were you making her do?"

"I wasn't making Helen *do* anything. Helen does what Helen wants to do. We all do, Kevin. That's how we get through life. Every day we make a choice to be here or not. The gutter was overflowing." His mother picked up the towel, retrieved her cigarette, and moved past him through the swinging door.

Kevin couldn't bring himself to return into the living room; instead he went out the back door. In the backyard, the rickety wood ladder lay across the grass.

He looked up to see the dripping gutter, righted the ladder, and leaned it against the house. He should climb up and remove the impasse of rotting brown leaves, but the heat of the afternoon was dense, immobilizing.

Therese stepped out from the back door.

"Do you want to get stoned?" asked Kevin instead of asking the question he actually needed answered.

Why Jude?

"Helen needs an X-ray. Her ankle is still swelling. Take her to the hospital."

"You take her to the hospital." Kevin ground his cigarette into the grass with his work boot.

"Why are you being such an idiot?"

"Shut up for once." Kevin took a step toward her, extending his hand until three of his fingers pressed against her lips.

Therese tried to look tough and unimpressed, but Kevin saw her frightened eyes wondering what else he might do.

"You're not strong enough to be alone? I'm alone," he said, pushing hard against her mouth. "You can handle it."

She smacked his hand away from her face.

"I'm pregnant."

Of course, thought Kevin. "I thought you couldn't get pregnant," he said out loud. "That's why you adopted a kid; you slept with Mark and Jude for years and never got pregnant."

"Yeah, and now I'm six months pregnant." Therese gleamed like wet metal in the sun. "Six months ago I wasn't sleeping with Mark or Jude. I was only with you."

Kevin's urge to get baked became suddenly acute.

The Three Graces

THERESE IS a tempest. Joy is a painter. Lisa is a playwright.

*

Therese is an adoptive mother. She's a widow.

When she arrived home from work her mother was wiping the kitchen table and her four-and-a-half-year-old son Aleksandar was driving a metal truck across the floor. He looked up and smiled and Therese smiled back.

"Why in God's name are you driving to Vermont this weekend?" asked her mother. "You're eight months pregnant. It's more than dangerous; it's stupid. At least let me come with you in case you go into labor."

"I'm not going to go into labor." Therese tried and failed not to sit down heavily.

"Your sister should be coming to Long Island to see you."

"Lisa invited me to Vermont to see her world, her life." Therese made a note to squeeze the sponge into the sink; her mother always left it on the way to mold. "Aleksandar needs to meet his Aunt Lisa!"

"Aleksandar's Aunt Lisa is old-fashioned rude." Her mother wound her scarf into a knot around her neck. "Driving to Vermont gives Lisa positive reinforcement. We should shun her for nine months. Let *her* see how it feels."

"That's your recommendation? Tit for tat?" Therese enjoyed appearing to take the high road.

"I'll be praying for you," her mother said, and then, under her breath, "even though it's your own damn fault if something happens." She slammed the door behind her.

Aleksandar climbed into Therese's lap, stretched his skinny arms around her belly. They hugged and hugged. Her mother didn't get it! The whole point of going to Vermont was to settle the score with her sister Lisa.

*

Joy is Lisa's friend. She's given birth as a surrogate.

At the Vermont arts center, Joy was completing a series of portraits in homage to the painter Alice Neel. Neel's life had been filled with children: lost and found, dead and alive, her own, her friends', her lovers'.

Joy was only interested in painting Jonathan.

Fourteen months had passed since Jonathan's birth, but rather than clarity and closure, Joy grew increasingly confused. Why had she agreed to be a surrogate for Marisa and Eugene? Not agreed, offered. Not offered, pushed. Marisa had been desperate enough to agree to it— surrogates were supposed to be younger than Joy, they were supposed to have had a previous healthy pregnancy and delivery prior to surrogacy, but Joy thought of herself as more powerful than other people, more capable, more able, and so did other people, perhaps in part because she was single by choice and bisexual and perhaps because she was clearly the most important person to herself. Herself and her work.

Friendly sympathy regarding Marisa and Eugene's devastation following their failed painful and expensive fertility treatments inspired an initial generosity that bloomed into something surprisingly seductive. Once the idea of "giving the gift of life" occurred to Joy, she could not let it go. She also began to believe as an artist it would be an instructive and incomparable experience to give birth.

When the original agreement was struck, Marisa and Eugene offered regular visits and routine involvement.

"He's *your* child," Joy insisted. "I'm just the final ingredient."

"Don't be silly," said Marissa. "You're essential."

"*We're* the ingredients," corrected Eugene. "You're the oven. Kidding!" he added, when Marissa glared.

Joy didn't know why she hadn't anticipated loss. After the birth Jonathan lived in Brooklyn with his parents, and at each subsequent visit, she felt increasingly unwelcome; it was then she decided to leave New York City for an extended residency at the Vermont arts center where several times a day she compulsively checked Marisa's Facebook to examine the photos that Marisa just as compulsively posted. Jonathan had Eugene's big eyes, Marisa's pointy chin.

One of these photos was the basis for the family portrait Joy was painting. It was to be another gift for Marisa and Eugene, but no matter what brushstrokes Joy employed, Eugene looked more like the leader of a motorcycle gang than a psychiatric social worker, while Marisa looked like an old Jackie Kennedy and Jonathan's furrowed brow made him look like a worried baby chimpanzee.

*

Lisa is a playwright. She's in recovery.

Lisa hauled a pot of warm water up the ladder to the tip of the A-Frame, to the triangular loft where she kept her computer, and where she was supposed to be writing her play. Cleaning in preparation for Therese and Aleksandar's impending visit felt as naïve and illusory as piling sandbags for a tsunami. Nonetheless she reached for cobwebs clinging to the walls. Her hands rubbed and rinsed while her mind replayed the late night calls she'd shared with Mark, Therese's husband, when he called post-fight with Therese.

"Lise?" Mark sounded so happy when Lisa picked up; he was usually high on something and she had usually been drinking. "Lise, are you awake? Do you have time to talk to me?" His plaintive need reeled her in, plus no one else had ever called her Lise. "I don't know how to treat your sister. I don't know how to keep her happy."

"I know, I know," Lisa murmured while succumbing to two of the most dangerous activities ever: comparing herself to Therese and falling for Mark.

Lisa was attractive. The adjective most often associated with Therese was gorgeous. Lisa had written several plays a small number of people had seen and admired, while Therese did real things with real people—she had a life—a husband, a house, a job. Now Therese even had a child of her own—the most grown-up thing of all.

Still, Mark had called *her*, Lisa—Lise! He thought of her; he needed her; he wanted her—though he'd never said these things exactly.

When, this past winter, Therese and Mark's adoption of Aleksandar became final, and Mark's late night phone calls ceased, Lisa told herself these things had nothing to do with her decision to go to Vermont for a residency at the arts center or to remain in Vermont after her residency was over. They had nothing at all to do with renting the A-Frame in the woods, never checking her personal email, letting her phone die, basically cutting all family ties.

Her mother had been the one to track her down, the letter arriving in summer in the A-Frame's rusty mailbox, her mother's familiar script in black ink.

Dear Lisa,
You know Therese adopted a child. But apparently you don't know her husband is dead. Mark had a heart attack in March. Dad and I are helping care for Aleksandar. Grow up and call me.
Love, Mom

Lisa had put her hand on the mailbox in order to remain standing. She'd crumpled her mother's letter, threw it into the woods, and banged her head against the metal box. The collection of skinny trees surrounding the A-Frame made no pretense of permanence. They seemed resigned. Once they grew large enough, yet again they would be cut down.

Lisa hadn't rushed back to New York, but she'd plugged in her phone, began checking her personal email occasionally, and written her mother asking her to relay a message of sympathy to Therese, and explaining she could not come home due to continued work on her play, as well as her work on maintaining sobriety, which was far easier in the Vermont woods than it would be in New York City.

Her mother's reply:

Dear Lisa,
Obviously you'll do whatever you want.
Love, Mom

When there were no more cobwebs left in the loft, Lisa turned on her computer. If pressed, she told the few people who inquired (her friend Joy and the people at AA meetings) that she was working on her new play, but in truth she spent most days walking the dirt roads that led away from and back to the A-Frame.

Now she opened the file containing her play-in-progress and read the unfinished lines. The words on the screen appeared exactly as they had the last time she'd opened the file; she was visiting her play, not writing it.

The label for her relationship with Mark—an emotional affair—had come to her only after it was over and she Googled it: an affair of the heart. A chaste infidelity. The fact that she'd invested so much energy in a fantasy filled her with shame.

Luckily, no one knew about it.

Also, she consoled herself, the capacity to imagine, to build a world out of nothing, was exactly the role of the playwright.

She descended the ladder with the water and the rags, and spent less than a minute sweeping the floor under the table and around the futon. The accumulated pile of dust, dirt and gravel she pushed onto a piece of thin cardboard, and chucked out the door.

*

In her rearview mirror, Therese watched Aleksandar yawn while playing with two plastic horses, saddled but cowboy-less; he had left the bow-legged men at home. She wondered if his propensity for hiding things had something to do with the almost four years he'd lived in the orphanage in Plovdiv, where at times there had not been enough toys and maybe shortages of food, attention, and affection.

She didn't know how he would respond to his soon-to-arrive brother or sister—she hadn't learned the baby's gender at the ultrasound because it seemed in keeping with the theme of the pregnancy: keep everybody guessing.

No one had come right out and asked her about the baby's father, but she had an answer ready: the baby belonged to her and to Aleksandar, though thus far Aleksandar had demonstrated zero interest in the baby despite her clear explanations (illustrated by children's books on the topic) of why her belly got bigger and bigger or the times she'd pulled his hand to feel the baby kicking. He'd only smiled blandly.

Now he was napping, mouth open, hands empty. It was only when he slept, or when she was at the law office where she worked as a paralegal, did she feel free enough to think about something other than what he might be feeling, thinking, or needing.

She exited off the main highway and began to drive through quaint Vermont towns. At the center of each were several spired churches and one square park, replete with a bandstand, the surrounding grass scattered with orange leaves. Framing the parks were white houses; Therese imagined wholesome inhabitants baking bread, sewing clothes, and reading books.

Soon the road became narrow, its surface changing from asphalt, to gravel, to dirt. Therese consulted the handwritten directions Lisa had scanned and sent as attachments. What kind of idiot chose to live in such a trashy rural area? Spindly trees filled the space between the road and ramshackle houses and trailers. Weeds grew up through rusted cars. A refrigerator lay on its side, detached door nearby.

A series of barking dogs ran toward the car. Aleksandar woke up and peered out the window. Therese put in a *Baby Reggae* CD and glanced at her phone. The signal was gone, just as Lisa had promised. The sky was beginning to darken.

Therese was looking for the proverbial fork in the road, where, according to Lisa's directions, she would veer right, and after six miles, "would see a red ribbon tied to a tree."

Lisa was such an ass! She thought her conversations with Mark were secret! Did she think Therese was not present in the house and/or deaf? When Mark was high he forgot to whisper. Therese had heard every word.

"Aleksandar." In the rearview mirror Aleksandar's eyes grew alarmed. Therese regretted her bright brittle tone. The next sentence would be softer, playful, fake. "Look for a red ribbon tied to a tree."

*

When the light wasn't good any more Joy quit painting and walked to the market. Due to its proximity to the arts center the market was stocked with gourmet items and always smelled like freshly ground coffee.

Joy selected crusty bread, locally produced butter, and a small jar of fleur de sel, deciding against a bouquet of white lilies because Lisa tended toward jealousy. In the past year Joy's paintings had begun to sell for "real money" as her gallerist put it. Making money from art had changed her relationship to art-making. She stopped considering, even subconsciously, whether she'd made the right decision to become an artist. Still, she did not want to appear rich and extravagant.

The small selection of wine next to the counter was well-curated. Joy decided Lisa's sobriety should be strong enough to have a glass of wine in her presence without pushing her off the wagon. She knew she shouldn't have accepted the invitation to dinner; she didn't like Lisa's sister, Therese. And the preschool aged child Therese had adopted from Bulgaria would be there too. Lisa wanted moral support. Joy also needed something, too, if not fortification at least a bit of pleasure. She chose a Côtes du Rhône.

The woman who rang her up had been leafing through People. A blurry photo of her family—her and her husband and four kids—was pinned to the bulletin board behind her. She noticed Joy looking.

"Grown now." The woman laughed. "All moved out, but still calling and caterwauling, needing this and that. It never ends."

Joy walked back to the arts center to get the keys to a Prius she was borrowing, looked up at the trees and the sky, felt the wind on her face. Usually the natural world was a balm, and a bottle of wine and loaf of bread in her hands would stimulate hunger, anticipation. She had always expected the best from life.

During Jonathan's birth, after his big head emerged, his round stomach seemed stuck for a moment, the labor and delivery nurses laughing with delight when he popped free. Marisa, weeping, had been first to hold him. Eugene, smiling beatifically, waited his turn. Joy felt the first prick of sorrow. Her intention was to bestow a gift. Instead she was bereft.

*

On the road in front of the A-Frame, the air was growing cold. Most of the birds had stopped chirping. Only the crows were still making noise. To keep warm, Lisa windmilled her arms in wide circles, did jumping jacks. No one knew how she was grieving for Mark, a man to whom she had absolutely no claim.

As she watched for a car she tried to envision the ways in which Mark's death may have changed Therese. Would her long curly hair be shorn? Perhaps it had turned white.

She imagined her sister looking ten years older, back curving forward like the stem of a heavy flower. Perhaps she had also gained weight.

Therese's imminent presence made Lisa thirsty. Oh my god, the taste of a gin martini. She prayed to her higher power while looking at the trees, a mix of conifers and hardwoods. Please, she said, please. This was the benefit of living in the woods: no easy access to alcohol. Not drinking made life so real it felt surreal.

She had been sober for nine months. It had been about the same amount of time since Therese had become a mother; six months since she'd become a widow. But who did what when and for how long and why didn't figure in to why Lisa had reached out to Therese to offer condolences and ask her to come to Vermont. It didn't make rational sense, but she missed and wanted to see her sister.

A car appeared, the driver's window rolling down.

"Holy Shit! We made it! Aleksandar, we found Auntie Lisa!" Therese got out of the car. Her hair was the usual cascade of highlighted curls. She wasn't hunched or stunted, but her midsection bulged. Lisa only closed her gaping mouth when Therese mimicked her dumbfounded expression.

"I'm pregnant," said Therese sweetly.

Lisa knew to be frightened whenever Therese was nice. She watched as her sister removed Aleksandar from his car seat and set him down on the road, a fine-boned dark-haired little boy. He gazed at the dusky woods. In each hand he held a plastic horse.

Lisa knelt down to hug him, but Aleksandar's body emitted a force field she respected. "Hi," she said instead. She generally thought of children as dumb, their edges as round as Thanksgiving Day Parade balloons. Aleksandar's shoulders were sharp, the features on his face precise. Lisa stood and turned to embrace Therese.

"I'm so sorry about Mark," she whispered into her sister's ear while trying to count—she was terrible at math—to see if the baby could be his. He died in March. It was October. "How many months are you?"

"Approximately eight. Do you like living in this shithole?" Therese's gesture encompassed the A-frame, the scraggly trees, the dirt road. Her profanity was as familiar and comforting as her floral perfume. Another car approached. Lisa had completely forgotten she'd invited Joy to join them for dinner.

*

Therese sat at the wooden table not far from the hearth with Aleksandar on her lap and chewed a piece of bread. The one room house reminded her of fairytales, dark at the edges, bright with fire in the middle. On the table were mismatched dishes, worn cloth napkins, an assortment of thrift shop forks. Lisa settled a frittata on a worn potholder in the middle of the table.

"Smells delicious." Joy opened the wine and poured herself a glass. Therese had met Joy many times over the years. Like most of Lisa's friends she was thin, her choppy hair expertly cut, her earrings bulky. Her black cashmere sweater was perfectly plain.

"Eggs, milk, cheddar, sweet potatoes, chives, and pepper." Lisa's list made Therese wonder if Joy had specific dietary restrictions.

"Mmm," said Joy as Lisa set a square of frittata onto her plate.

Lisa had been envious of Joy for years, and always went on and on about Joy's wonderful paintings. Therese was sure Lisa had told her about Mark, not just his death, but his drug use, and his and Therese's terrible marriage.

"Joy, you know Lisa isn't drinking, right?" asked Therese.

"I'm fine," said Lisa.

"Yes of course," said Joy. "But wine exists and people bring it to dinner parties. I didn't know you were pregnant. Congratulations—I don't think I said that yet."

"I'm *fine*." Lisa placed a sizzling piece of frittata onto Therese's plate. "Eat."

"Thank you, *Lise*." Therese reached out and pinched Lisa's forearm as hard as she could.

"Hey!" said Lisa. "That hurt!"

Therese felt a brief rip of satisfaction along with the ache of her sciatic nerve. Such a long day of driving. Yes, *Lise*, I know about you and Mark! You should pay for going behind my back! A year ago Therese would have yelled this out loud, but Aleksandar sat on her lap, still too shy for his own chair. His bony butt dug into her thighs. The baby's repetitive kicks felt wearisome, a child yanking her hand, a little taste of parenting two children.

"Thanks to Joy," said Lisa, "we have bread and butter and fleur de sel." The red pinch mark on her arm had already begun to fade.

"And wine," muttered Therese. Men often paid Joy more attention than she was worth, but Joy was one of very few women who didn't seem to need men and obviously this made her even more compelling to them. "Bringing alcohol into Lisa's house probably isn't the best idea?"

Joy took a long sip of Côtes du Rhône. Aleksandar reached toward her shimmering emerald earrings, then withdrew his hand.

"God Therese, shut up!" said Lisa through mouth full of frittata.

Therese buttered and salted a slice of bread; the salt made the butter taste so sweet.

*

Joy saw Therese pinch Lisa, and felt Lisa's panic, but she was too astonished to say or do anything about it. An only child, she found sibling behavior bizarre. She took another long sip of wine.

"Lisa," Therese's tone was probing, ready to pounce, "did you finish writing your play?"

"I've come to terms with not finishing my play right now," said Lisa.

Therese blatantly rolled her eyes.

"It's a process," offered Joy. She resented direct interrogation of artists by non-artists.

"I'm simply living in Vermont," said Lisa. "That's it. I live here."

"What do you do all day if you aren't writing?" asked Therese.

"I take walks," said Lisa.

"You can't walk in New York?" asked Therese.

"A break can be so helpful." Joy noticed how many physical qualities the sisters shared: foreheads, noses, lips, chins, shoulders.

"Joy, you don't take breaks," said Lisa. "You work all the time."

Joy also saw something gestural. Lisa and Therese held their heads at similar angles, moved their hands in similar ways when they spoke.

"I take short breaks." Neither of the sisters seemed to be listening when she spoke.

"A playwright has to cast a spell," said Lisa, "and right now I feel powerless to do so."

"Are you still drinking?" Therese cut a piece of frittata with her fork.

"Yeah, I'm drinking water! Here." Lisa thrust the basket at Therese. "Have more bread."

"Therese, how are you doing?" Joy poured herself another glass of wine. "I was so sorry to hear about Mark."

"You're very kind," said Therese tonelessly, as if the condolence was expected and unappreciated. "What are *you* painting these days, Joy?"

Joy knew Therese intended to sound dismissive. Was it her pregnancy, the fact that she had adopted a child, or her husband's death that she thought gave her permission to be casually cruel?

"Portraits. People. I'm exploring loss."

"What exactly did you lose?" Therese's voice was sticky.

Aleksandar looked up from his plate in alarm.

That's right, thought Joy. Your mom is waging war.

"A baby," said Joy. Each word seemed to weigh several pounds.

"Are you finished for now, Aleksandar?" asked Therese. "Do you want to be excused?" The boy slipped off her lap. Therese pulled a plastic character from her bag—Puss in Boots. "Do you want to play with your cat? I have your horses too. It's warm on the rug. Just don't get too close to the fire." Aleksandar lay down on his stomach and lined up his toys so they were facing him. The fire flickered behind them. Therese leaned as forward as her belly would allow. "Did you have a miscarriage?" she asked quietly.

"Lisa didn't tell you I was a surrogate mother for my friends Marisa and Eugene?"

"I thought I told you." Lisa looked stricken.

"No, Lisa didn't tell me anything. You know Aleksandar is adopted, right?" whispered Therese. "From Bulgaria?"

Joy knew her own statement of fact about being a surrogate could not rationally be construed as an attack on Therese's decision to complete a foreign adoption, but like most women, she was used to the constant seesaw of judging and being judged and detected the note of warning in Therese's voice.

"I know." Joy smiled in Aleksandar's direction. He was moving the cat and horses around on the rug, saying something she couldn't quite hear. She got the feeling he was outlining rules for the game and naming the consequences for breaking them.

"You gave your friends an incredible gift." Therese grimaced after saying this. Joy was certain that since Mark's death, people offered her similar platitudes.

"No." Joy placed her elbows on the table, rested her chin in her hands. "I made a terrible mistake."

"You don't mean that!" Lisa's mouth was full of egg. "You don't make mistakes, Joy! You're brilliant!"

"Shut up, Lisa," said Therese. "Of course she means it."

"I thought I could have a baby and give it away without pain," said Joy.

"That's such bullshit," said Therese.

"Why is it bullshit?" challenged Lisa.

"There's no life without pain," snapped Therese.

Lisa's mouth dropped open. Joy realized her own expression was the same, as if she and Lisa were the sisters, a pair of shocked and clueless little girls.

"That's so true," said Joy finally. "And now you're pregnant."

She wasn't sure why she said this.

"I know," said Therese. "Lisa, newsflash: I'm getting married at Christmas. You have to come home."

"What are you talking about?" Lisa got up and began stacking empty plates.

"I'm marrying Jude. An old friend of mine," Therese clarified for Joy's benefit.

"They've been sleeping together for years," Lisa further clarified. "Is Jude the father, Therese? And didn't you hear me? I said I need to stay in Vermont."

"It's getting late," said Joy. "I should go."

Lisa's smile was weak, directed toward no one.

"Take the wine with you," demanded Therese.

Aleksandar looked so content on the rug in front of the fire, so immersed in the world of his toys, that Joy chose not to give him a perfunctory farewell. He would soon have a sibling; he would have practice, it would shape him, like a kid forced to learn how to play piano whether he liked it or not.

The Prius she'd borrowed from one of the sculptors was parked on the road just beyond the ribbon Lisa had tied to a tree; in the dark it was no longer visible. On her trip to the A-Frame Joy had passed many such markers: deflated balloons, bedraggled plastic flowers, decomposing pieces of cardboard. Weddings, bonfires, yard sales. People put up these signs so carefully, but never bothered to take them down.

The Dark Side of the Moon

PAUL LIVED at a modernist remove, people separate from the divine. He never told his wife Alice he was clairvoyant, though she believed in miracles, water into wine, loaves and fishes, Lazarus. (And he wouldn't be surprised if Woolf or Proust indulged in the occult.)

In the month of November the sun went down early. Paul took his meds in the morning and looked forward to the evening's warming ritual: summery vodka tonic, bowl of smoked nuts, circles of light cast on the carpet by living room lamps. Alice sat next to him on the couch.

"I can do the math." A necklace of big amber beads stood out against her sweater. Alice always made the effort to look nice, even when it was just the two of them. "Mark was alive in March."

Paul crunched an almond. Order, symmetry, neatness, bourgeois prudishness. He didn't begrudge Alice the various reasons why she believed their son-in-law Mark was the father of their daughter Therese's soon-to-be-born child. Mark was dead now, but alive at the time of conception.

The door to the hospital room was open. From the hallway Paul witnessed the archetypal tableau. The Family. Therese, sitting up in bed, eyes bright, curly hair flattened, cheekbones splotched. Jude, Mark's friend from high school, unshaven, blue oxford shirt untucked and unbuttoned at the neck, sleeves rolled up to the elbows. Newborn Annabelle lying in her mother's lap, facing her mother, body and head and even part of her forehead wrapped tightly. Eyes closed, lips pressed together.

Though an atheist, Paul felt affinity with Updike's helpless, hapless, hopeful, just-past-mid-century white men, Updike's command of the language so assured, so fleet and fast, Paul knew he believed God really did love him, and Rabbit, too.

From behind the wall of Alice's back, good energy bounced around the hospital room. Paul reminded himself not to trust it. He'd felt fear as they drove to the hospital, the fear increasing as he found a parking spot and walked behind Alice through the halls to find labor and delivery. Alice tried to hide what she called her "negativity" but he felt that too. Their fear was rational. They never knew if Therese would be mean to them, and just how mean, all the while hoping she would be nice.

"Annabelle looks like a little nun!" Alice spoke so freely, so carelessly. Paul waited for the bomb to go off, but Therese laughed. Alice's dolman-sleeved coat flowed behind her as she swooped to kiss Therese and Annabelle and twirled to embrace Jude. All without asking if she could hold the baby. True restraint.

Paul shook Jude's hand. He was no longer the callow youth Paul remembered from the 1980s who'd hung around with Mark and another guy, a kid named Kevin, now a plumber; they'd been the three musketeers. Jude had changed, so what, Paul still had the urge to punch him. Instead he bent to kiss his daughter and granddaughter. Annabelle, Annabelle. He loved her name. He loved her! She looked just like Therese's older sister Lisa did when she was born. Best not to mention it.

"Did I tell you I had a natural birth?" Therese, shy and proud, her face puffy, the aftermath of exertion, the evidence of her primal experience.

"Wonderful!" Alice's advice prior to the delivery had been "Demand every drug they can give you." She sat down on the edge of the bed; Therese passed the baby. "Hello sweetheart," Alice cooed. "I love you. Yes, I do."

Jude's once angular face was soft from witnessing the birth, but also from the weight he'd gained. His chubbiness made him look friendly, dad-like, but Paul didn't love Jude, and wouldn't love Jude. Jude was one of those guys who put himself first as a matter of course. The most essential qualification for fatherhood was sacrifice.

Paul reminded himself to stay on guard, and sent a telepathic message to Alice to do the same; he spent a fair amount of time sending Alice messages that never made it. She looked as happy now as she had on their wedding day. The joy of Annabelle's birth had changed them all for the better. Paul knew it was temporary.

The day after Therese was released to go home from the hospital with the baby, Paul drove over to help out. He didn't tell Alice he was going, because Alice was at work and afterwards would go to Trader Joe's where she'd dawdle tasting free samples. If he'd told Alice he was going to see Therese, she'd have wanted to come, and would have insisted he wait for her, but he couldn't wait. He'd felt bereft ever since leaving the hospital.

The spot in front of Therese's house was occupied by a beige

Cadillac belonging to Mark's father, Adam. Adam had made life hard on Mark with all his rah rah hard work businessman bullshit. God knows Therese had been hard on Mark too. And in a sense she was continuing to be hard on him. Not even a year after Mark's death, she was planning to marry Jude.

Paul had wholeheartedly approved when Therese married Mark. He wanted grandchildren and was beginning to see Lisa, a playwright, would remain "child free." Paul knew Mark from when he was a kid in the neighborhood. In high school Mark had become Therese's boyfriend. They were on and off for years until they married.

Adult Mark was handsome, a successful stockbroker. He handled Alice expertly, treating her as an intimate while simultaneously managing to keep her at arm's length. Plus there was the matter of the peace he kept with Therese, which simply meant they stayed married. Therese was always pissed off about something he did or didn't do. Mark became the object (or subject, it went back and forth) of Therese's sporadic rage. Once she married Mark, she didn't fight with Paul and Alice (over nothing) quite as much. Paul felt guilty about that then. More so now.

"Mark was the son you never had," Alice said to him after Mark overdosed. Mark had been a drug addict and Therese's emotional punching bag, but never his own son. Mark belonged to Adam.

Paul saw Mark's tendency toward self-destruction as the curse of being sensitive—this ability to so clearly perceive what others missed. Growing up Paul had been told, "you're too sensitive" and "toughen up." Alice found his sensitivity alternately wonderful—her own mother had been outright abusive—and annoying. Feeling so much made him inconsistently manly.

After Mark's death, Alice lamented about not having been able to see that his life would end the way it did. An overdose in the basement.

"We were deceived, we were fooled!"

Paul did not say: I knew. I knew and I didn't protect him because I couldn't. I couldn't protect him the way you protect me. He did not add what he knew was the truth about life: life was going to get some people. If it weren't for the meds and for Alice who was always shoring him up… Paul knew all along what was coming for Mark.

He rang Therese's doorbell. Adam opened the door with Aleksandar hanging onto his pant leg making funny faces.

"*Mazel tov.*" Adam squeezed harder and longer than Paul during any handshake. "Congratulations. Once again you're a grandfather." Yes, Adam was a scorekeeper; Aleksandar's adoption from an orphanage in Bulgaria had been completed the month before Mark died.

"Same to you," Paul lied.

"Come in, come in." Adam was the Kingly archetype. He acted like whatever house he happened to be in *belonged* to him. True, he and his now-departed wife Miriam gave Mark and Therese the down payment for this house.

Adam employed phrases that circumscribed people, that limited and reduced them to a slot, put them in their places, like "higher up the food chain." He thought of himself as "alpha." All the business types did this—slaughtered language with their jargon—like using impact as a verb.

"Stay away from my daughter!" Paul wanted to shout. Instead he crouched down and gathered his grandson in a hug. "Congratulations to the big brother! How come you're not at school?"

"Life Saver?" Aleksandar's lips tickled Paul's ear and his hands pulled at Paul's pocket. Paul extracted the candy. Aleksandar pried off two candies.

"Two!" Paul pretended to be horrified. "Cherry *and* orange?"

"Cherry and orange," repeated Aleksandar, candy already in his mouth. Therese and Mark had had their worries about adopting a four-year-old. They'd been worried about attachment, about language, about overall development. Paul had visions of the orphanage in Plovdiv; no abuse *per se*, but perhaps benign neglect. It was a wonder anyone survived childhood or parents. Look how Lisa and Therese had turned out. Paul was buoyed by Aleksandar's sly confidence.

"A little early for candy." Adam stood straddle-legged in Therese's living room. As if Paul were the interloper. Adam served in Vietnam, while Paul was (thankfully) declared unfit, he'd been hospitalized twice for depression in high school, zapped with electric. Adam believed in law and order, Paul in peace and love. Paul canvassed for McGovern. Adam voted for Nixon.

"I like candy *all* the time," said Aleksandar.

Paul forced himself not to stagger as he straightened up. Suck in your gut, he told himself. Alice called it "using your core muscles." After thirty-eight years of marriage his brain and Alice's were basically fused, which was why it was surprising she didn't receive his telepathy or see his visions.

"He didn't want to go to kindergarten today," said Adam, "and Therese didn't force him."

"Adam!" yelled Therese from the kitchen. "Leave him alone!"

Paul felt it: Adam wanted to take Mark's place. Instead of punching Adam in the face, he cupped Aleksandar's chin. If he'd known he was going to be home from school, he would have brought him a little toy.

"It's not so easy to be a big brother, is it?" Paul offered more Life Savers.

"That's too much sugar," said Adam as Aleksandar shoved candy into his mouth.

"Dad! Come in here! Annabelle just woke up!" called Therese.

Aleksandar made his "monster" face by rigidly sticking out his tongue.

"*Bubaleh*," said Adam. "That's not nice."

"You should have seen Lisa when Therese was born," said Paul as the three of them walked to the kitchen. "Hi, my girl," he said, kissing Therese on the top of her head. "I thought you might be all by your lonesome." He didn't intend to sound wistful.

"Lisa was horrible to me!" Therese was sitting in a rocking chair bought by Adam, looking pleased with herself, and why shouldn't she be? Annabelle was in her arms. The chair was actually a glider cushioned in sky blue velvet. There was a matching hassock, and on the hassock rested Therese's bare feet, toenails painted orange.

"You know how it is," said Paul. "Classic sibling rivalry."

"Mark was an only child," said Adam. "But I had a brother, now deceased."

"Oh yeah, it was bad," Paul said finally after failing to think of a consoling way to respond. "Older siblings can't help feeling displaced. And this guy," Paul scooped up Aleksandar and lifted him until Aleksandar pedaled in the air. Paul wanted the little boy to look down on Adam. "This guy has already been through a lot." Paul put him down; the kid was heavy. "How's life with the baby, Aleksandar?"

"The baby cries." Aleksandar made a face. "She smells. She doesn't do nothing."

"Anything," said Adam. "She doesn't do anything."

"You love the baby," said Therese.

"Nothing nothing," muttered Aleksandar. He was holding fists out at his sides.

"But now Lisa and Therese have each other," said Paul.

"Yeah right," said Therese drily.

Lisa. A whole other story. In the patch of yard visible through the window over the sink, Paul saw a bright red cardinal. Aleksandar marched over to his mother, grabbed Annabelle's foot, shook it.

"Gentle with your sister." Therese put an arm around Aleksandar, pulled him close and kissed him. "Dad, do you want to hold the baby?"

Therese and Aleksandar went into the living room to play checkers and Paul settled into the glider with the baby, still swaddled, but today her head was uncovered, tuft of black hair exposed. Annabelle's eyes were open but unfocused and slightly dissatisfied in a way he remembered from Lisa. For the first month of her life, Lisa seemed to still have a foot in the time and place before being born.

Therese was born two weeks past her due date; she came into the world as robust and fully present as a linebacker.

Paul glided while Adam stood at the sink, a towel stuck into the waistband of his trousers, minuscule soap bubbles lifting into the air above his head before popping. The pleasant scent of lemon dishwashing liquid filled the kitchen. Annabelle fell back to sleep. Her eyelids began to twitch, as if she were dreaming. Paul closed his eyes too. What a gift to hold a new human whose life was countable in days.

Paul had lived sixty-four *years*. When that Beatles song came out he'd been twenty. Instead of Vietnam, he'd gone to Library School. Friends who managed to come home put their uniforms and medals away—there'd been no parades. They'd been spit on, called murderers. Paul knew his pain was lesser. When *Dark Side of the Moon* came out he flipped the record over and over. Anthony Barbario, Eddie Simeone, George Stone, pals from high school, dead and gone forever. Depression was a constant push from behind, or a nudge as he sat at his desk. Or it bobbed alongside him while he swam in the ocean, or bumped against his shoulders as he stood on a crowded bus.

He and Alice never talked about his depression with the girls; the times it was bad when they were growing up they'd pretended he had the flu. This memory, spring or summer, they weren't wearing coats—they were walking into church, Alice holding one girl and Paul the other, Alice in a pretty blouse and skirt and heels—pure and fresh and gorgeous. The girls wore pink and yellow dresses, cloth diapers hidden beneath frilly white rubber pants. He'd barely managed to get out of bed the dread that morning had been overwhelming, his hands had shaken so badly shaving he'd nicked himself again and again. Finally the bleeding had stopped. His painful reality neatly hidden beneath suit and tie. Alice made sure he was dapper. Everyone's eyes upon them in the church. Poor saps, he thought, feeling their envy. They were coveting his wife, his daughters, his life.

"Hey, Paul."

"Yeah?" Paul must have nodded off.

"How many more years before you retire?" The dishes Adam washed were dripping on the wooden rack next to the sink, the towel once again hanging over the towel rack.

"Mouths to feed."

"What?" demanded Adam.

Paul realized he was still gliding, holding Annabelle. He didn't see anything for her yet, a blessing. It wasn't right both his girls were flawed. For Lisa it was alcohol, for Therese it was men.

"How many more years do plan to work?" Adam's voice a drill, insistent.

"At least five." Paul told himself to pull it together. "I'll be seventy."

Adam pulled over a kitchen chair and sat down. "I'm not sure how prudent Mark was with money," he murmured. "Have you spoken to Therese?"

"Things will work out one way or another."

Adam sighed impatiently. A spurt of shame zipped through Paul. He knew Therese's financial situation; he didn't have to ask. It made him anxious to think about it, so he'd stopped thinking about it.

"You're her father. It's your job to ask her about money."

Paul didn't answer. Annabelle was still asleep. The game of checkers was taking a turn for the worse in the living room.

"No!" Aleksandar was yelling. "No! No!"

"I'm going to cuddle you," answered Therese, as if it were a threat. "I'm going to cuddle you!"

"Therese is a grown woman," said Paul. He also didn't want to say the bad news out loud: Therese was broke.

Adam had no idea it had taken him decades to develop empathy for the still imperfect man he was today, as well as for the skinny husband and father he had been, working at the New York City Public Library. In the early seventies the city had borrowed money, hoping the failing economy (falling tax receipts, decline of manufacturing, white flight to suburbs) would change for the better, and later, hoping the federal government would bail them out. The federal government didn't bail them out. Credit to New York City was cut off. Thus began the endless rounds of "budget cuts." The streets were rutted. The garbage sat. There were fewer librarians, fewer teachers, fewer cops.

Paul was sure Adam had called for austerity; Adam was the type of guy who called necessities amenities. Paul was the type of guy who instead of getting a second job in the evening to augment his salary, put on his headphones and zoned out. The shit with Nixon had happened again with Reagan. Then came the Bushes. Yes, Obama had secured a second term, but Paul knew what was to come after that. Jesus Christ. He didn't tell a soul, not even Alice. The knowledge was his burden. Plus swear to god, no one would believe it.

"Maybe Alice can talk to Therese about her finances?" Adam was a dog with a bone. Paul berated himself. Of course it was obvious Alice protected him. How had he made his wife's life better? She was still working, too, as a secretary at a middle school, perpetually learning a new program for the computer, hitting the wrong buttons, emails bouncing back.

"I can talk to Alice if you don't want to." Adam often acted annoyed by Alice, but Paul knew he was charmed. In this competition only Paul was on top: Adam had married a Miriam, God rest her soul. It wasn't worth the mental energy of a comparison.

He had married Alice. Alice was constant catharsis. Alice said what she thought. She did what she liked. She wasn't careful. She didn't apologize. She had been so glowing in her youth. Radiant! He'd been stunned when she agreed to marry him.

"Two children will be expensive," said Adam.

"I suppose I know that more so than you," muttered Paul as Annabelle opened her eyes. Her blue eyes would soon turn brown.

"It's my duty to take care of Mark's children."

Annabelle looked like Lisa right now, plain and simple, but pretty soon it wouldn't be so simple; she would look like Jude, too.

"I'm setting up a trust for each of the children." Adam was a goddamn train on a track!

"Good," said Paul, and hoped that was the end of it.

From the living room came the sound of checkers hitting the wall.

"Stop it, Aleksandar!" yelled Therese. Annabelle let out a tremulous wail.

"No!" yelled Aleksandar. "No!" His new favorite word.

Paul gathered the baby closer to his chest in an attempt to comfort her. "Therese and Jude and the children can come and live with me and Alice," he told Adam. Life with young children would once again be exhilarating and treacherous, like being in the ocean. You could never turn your back.

"They'll live with me," said Adam. "I'm not working. I can watch the children during the day. I can hire help."

"Aleksandar!" yelled Therese. "Stop hitting me!"

"I have the larger house," Adam said before leaving the kitchen.

Paul used his muscles to get up from the glider with Annabelle in his arms. He felt relieved and relaxed. Finally. *This* was his girl, this was typical Therese, this was Therese to a T: yelling when both her children were screaming. And then suddenly it was just Annabelle.

In the living room, Therese was sitting on the floor with Aleksandar in her lap, her arms wrapped tightly around him.

"You're safe," she repeated firmly as she rocked him back and forth, "you're safe." Aleksandar sucked his thumb. "Hold the baby closer, dad," she snapped. "She needs to feel secure."

"Give her to me," said Adam.

Paul hugged Annabelle against his chest. She was squirmy, hot, pure energy, pure power. "Flesh of my flesh!" He sent the message to Annabelle. Voila! Maybe she had the gift/curse as well? She stopped crying.

"Listen you two," said Therese. "Kevin is Annabelle's father. He signed the Acknowledgement of Paternity at the hospital."

"Kevin? Mark's old friend from high school?" asked Paul.

"The plumber?" asked Adam. "Impossible."

"Yeah, Kevin," said Therese. "Jude will adopt Aleksandar. Annabelle's father is Kevin. I know because I slept with him." For a moment the only sound in the room was Aleksandar sucking his thumb. "By then I wasn't sleeping with Mark," she added.

"That's a disgusting habit, Aleksandar." Adam plunked down on the couch. "Get your hand out of your mouth."

"Leave him alone." Therese spoke in such a level tone Paul understood it was a warning. He wondered what had prevented him from seeing the truth about Kevin. The moment they were in wasn't modern; it was post. Post-modernists didn't place the highest value on unity. They didn't lament the broken world, they laughed in its face while they played with the pieces.

"Adam," said Therese. "Stop looking at me like that." Paul got it when he looked again at his daughter on the floor, Aleksandar in her lap, her multi-color curls springing in all directions. Therese was the right woman for this moment—she thrived on chaos.

Denouement

ON THE train from Vermont to New York, Lisa watched snow-covered trees blur together.

Therese's voicemail was emphatic. It gained momentum.

THERESE: You're still sober, right? I want you to officiate my wedding. I mean our wedding—Jude's and mine. You can become a minister online. Shut your eyes for a minute and visualize yourself standing in Mom and Dad's living room in front of the television, the rest of us in a semicircle, facing you. Only the essential people will be there: you, Mom and Dad, Jude's mother, his sister Joanna. I invited Mark's dad, too, but Adam won't come, right? That would be weird. Kevin is Jude's best man. This is your chance to make amends. Don't you have to? Isn't it one of the steps? Don't think I don't miss Mark. Remember that game we played as kids? The one where you sat on my chest? I feel like that. And Mark doesn't always feel gone. He feels like smoke, vanishing when you reach for it. You can wear whatever you want to the wedding. Think about Mom. No, don't think about Mom! She'll kill the fatted calf for you! Seriously, we're getting a really nice caterer. Don't judge me. Jude's good for me. Aleksandar needs a father. Annabelle has Kevin. In case you missed it? This is life I'm talking about, Lisa. You're my sister, and I need you.

For Therese, thought Lisa, Mark had been primarily a body, a tall muscular husband-body, grinning, excusing itself on mysterious errands, returning hyper or subdued, while for her Mark had morphed from inconsequential brother-in-law into significant disembodied other, a voice on the phone consistently wry, needy, high on one thing or another.

When Mark first began to call her, she listened to his circular logic with tolerant detachment. Too soon she began to anticipate his calls like a lover. Then he was dead. He'd been dead nine months.

In the past week, Lisa had broken the lease on the A-frame, sold her truck, and kicked out the sub-letter from her Hell's Kitchen apartment. In addition to fear (how was she even remotely qualified to officiate a wedding?) she felt a pang of loss. She missed the drafty A-frame she'd rented after her residency at the Vermont arts center was over. She missed Vermont. Before selling the truck she'd made one final trip to the spring to fill an empty plastic gallon jug, which now sloshed overhead in the luggage rack.

Snow continued to fall, but the weather seemed to matter less as the train moved further south, and the cities clustered closer together.

Lisa lugged the water onto the subway, and up four flights of stairs. The studio had been left surprisingly neat: French Press rinsed and upside down on the dish rack, bare mattress on the bed, sheets washed and folded on top of folded wool blankets; the bathroom had been scrubbed.

She found the silver flask in the closet. Even after washing it with hot water and soap, it smelled like gin, but she filled it with water from the spring, and stashed it into her handbag; she would sip whenever tempted. Before living in the A-frame, the studio had felt cozy, not claustrophobic. After several big swigs from the flask, she realized she must ration the water, and in addition, find a meeting to attend. Meetings and water would not be enough to keep her sober, not in New York City, not when she was about to go back to work.

Another ritual was necessary.

The process of bundling up was the same as it had been in Vermont, but instead of stepping onto the A-frame's porch, and through the winter bare yard to a dirt road lined with scraggly trees, there was a dim hallway, sour stairs, West 48th Street. She walked until she crossed the West Side Highway and stood at the railing to watch the Hudson until daylight disappeared.

BACK TO WORK

Persons in the Play

Lisa: *thirty-nine year old white female playwright from Long Island, adjunct instructor City College Department of Theater and Speech, recovering alcoholic, attractive, anxious. Wears a gray wool shift dress, lavender tights, John Fluevog shoes.*

Anthony: *twenty-nine year old Black playwright, adjunct instructor City College Department of Theater and Speech, gay, from Newark, New Jersey. Handsome. Trousers and blazer are fashionably small bright and tight.*

The Place

"Theater B" a 200-seat theater in Aaron Davis Hall on the City College Campus in New York City.
At rise, Lisa is sitting on a stool center stage, facing the house. Anthony sits in the front row. On stage a dim blue light rotates.

ANTHONY: How many actors are we talking about?
LISA: Three, but one's a kid.
ANTHONY: You're asking for it with a kid.
LISA: An adolescent.
ANTHONY: Better. Boy or girl? Or?
LISA: Any of the above.
ANTHONY: Director will fuck that right up.
LISA: Just one of many "choices" they'll have to make.
(The two of them cackle for a minute.)
ANTHONY: So you don't get to choose? The Department is naming a director?
LISA: Somebody from Hunter.
ANTHONY: No, they did not. A Hunter bitch? *(Another round of laughter.)*
LISA: I should have written a grant. Found a professional venue.
ANTHONY: This is a good space.
LISA: I was lazy. I should have found a stage with even the tiniest bit of cachet.
ANTHONY: Keep the risk low, that's what I heard you say.
LISA: I should have, I should have. "Don't should on yourself." That's what we say in AA. I'm almost forty.
ANTHONY: You're getting back on your feet.
LISA: This is one step away from a student production!
ANTHONY: Yup.

LISA: You haven't told me what you've been up to.
ANTHONY: Nope.
LISA: I see you on the Twitters, Anthony. I know about your Playwriting Fellowship at La Mama.
ANTHONY: When your play is ready, take it to the Kitchen or Here or the Flea. One day at a time, remember?
LISA: Shut the fuck up, Sweet Anthony, just shut the fuck up.

After leaving the theater, Lisa stopped by the part-time faculty office. She expected it to be empty because even when classes were in session instructors avoided it, partially because the wedged-in cast off furniture reminded them they weren't on tenure track, but mostly because they were busy. Adjuncts taught at three or more schools to add to the grants, awards, and fellowships that helped them cobble together a life in the theater.

The party line was resentment at "having to teach," but Lisa suspected others found, as she did, the connection with young ambitious eager desperate gorgeous students sustaining. She sat on a desk, and used her phone to find an AA meeting; one started in nearby Harlem in an hour. On a bulletin board hung shared and defaced syllabi (*Introfuckion to Theater*) along with postings from the Part-Time Instructors Union, including information about Food Stamps. Good. She could apply online.

All along Amsterdam Ave. she counted bars. Macaleer's Pub, The Lion's Head Tavern, Jake's Dilemma, The Tangled Vine. The AA meetings held all day every day across the city were outnumbered by the bars. And in the bars such a pleasing variety of barstools: vinyl-covered, low-backed wood faux colonial, minimalist metal, translucent Lucite. The AA meeting was in a church basement, the fluorescent-lit room filled with the same tan metal folding chairs found at every meeting she'd ever attended.

Her chair grew warm from her body, and she began to feel at home.

On Christmas Eve morning, the day of Therese's wedding, Lisa refilled her flask with the last bit of water from the spring. She skipped her walk to the Hudson, instead walking to Penn Station to catch a train to her parents' house. In the night it had snowed. Sidewalks and crosswalks were crusty with ice, or slushy. Walking with the throngs headed south on Eighth Avenue at ten a.m. was the opposite of her Zen pilgrimage west on 48th Street at dusk.

Over her dress she wore her ex's tweed coat. Being back on social media meant she knew Larry had recently married a twenty-seven year old in pharmaceutical sales who enjoyed hiking and, "movies that make me smile long after the credits roll." Lisa's expensive snow boots would not have been affordable had they not been on sale, and a size too big. She'd forgotten wool socks. Her feet in tights slipped and rubbed.

Close to Penn Station, she paused in front of a bar whose neon sign glowed OPEN. You didn't need a grant or fellowship, a degree or award, a producer or director. In this particular establishment, she'd drunk many gin martinis. Drinking helped her pause, relax, and take pleasure in what so often felt like sad, frightening, chaotic life. Liquor wasn't in fact affirming, it was merely predictable: she knew what the first glorious martini felt like, as well as the less-glorious second. She drank the third, fourth, and fifth at home so instead of slipping off a stool, she could fall into bed.

She pulled the flask from her bag. People swarmed around her, one woman looking back over her shoulder and gazing compassionately at Lisa as she tilted her flask.

"It's water!" yelled Lisa, but the woman had already disappeared into the crowd.

Lisa continued walking, making a quick inventory of her positives. Technically she had a play in development. Her skin was good, she was still relatively thin, and she felt a clarity at thirty-nine-and-three-quarters she had not felt at twenty-five. She descended the stairs at Penn Station telling herself to be nice to herself. This was a new, sober, approaching-forty thing, seeing herself as a separate person, one deserving of love and care. Be gentle with yourself was a corny thing to say, but she said it.

After purchasing a round-trip ticket to Lawnhurst, she stood in front of the board flipping numbers and letters like an old clock radio, and waited with the other commuters headed to Long Island.

In the *New York Times*, a theater critic complained about contemporary playwrights using the technique of direct address far too frequently. Lisa too, felt the urge to explain:

LISA: My younger sister Therese, and my mother, Alice, were louder and more dramatic. They sucked up my father's attention. My father and I barely spoke. In college at SUNY Purchase I'd learned this lack of relationship constituted a problem. I went home for a long weekend, and at breakfast the morning I was to return to school, asked my father to meet me for lunch at Penn Station, where I'd switch from the Long Island Rail Road to MetroNorth. My father looked at his gatekeeper. My mother nodded. I named a place we could meet.

When I arrived in Penn Station's main concourse later that morning wearing a plaid miniskirt, black tights, combat boots, and a red sweater, cold and then hot air whooshed past, the rising odor of donuts, coffee, perfume, cigarettes, pine cleanser, and beneath all that, urine. People gathered, dispersed. A cloud of cigarette smoke floated near the ceiling. I maneuvered through the crowd, my suitcase banging against my legs. I'd packed in a state of vigorous euphoria; I was to have lunch alone with my father. In addition I was sleeping with two young men. The chatty RA on my hall who slipped into my room uninvited yet welcome. He moaned so loudly I had to pinch him in order to continue pretending we weren't disturbing my roommate. Like my father, Mack, my skinny stoner from New Hampshire said next to nothing. He and I made no conversation, had nothing in common, experienced zilch rapport. As a campus party wound down, Mack would find me. The deliriously quiet hours I spent with him involved him crouching over me, trailing his blond hair back and forth across my bare stomach. "Take a shower with me," were among his few spoken words. I issued long-winded refusals because I imagined showering with Mack somehow so pleasurable I might explode. He always nudged me out of his bed before daybreak, ignoring me later in the cafeteria, looking past me, through me, leaving me exquisitely wounded.

There were ten minutes until I was to meet my father; just enough time to pee. The Penn Station women's bathroom existed, existentially, at an even greater depth than the subway tracks, and I joined the line of women, either unsuspecting or all too vividly remembering the stench, the oily oscillating fan, the broken rusted dripping sinks, the tiny, wrinkled crone who condemned the woman whose turn had arrived by pointing to a coffin-like stall. Young, old, rich, poor: all women felt New York at its most devastating when she had to pee (or worse) in transit. Thus we made this hellish pit stop. I set my suitcase on the floor next to the toilet, cursing the women who peed standing up, spraying urine all over the seat.

In the appointed restaurant, I sat on a swiveling stool facing the concourse, and waited for my dad. A young man, long coat flapping, walked past. It was Dave, a guy on whom I'd had a maudlin high school crush. He walked by again from the other direction, and entered the restaurant.

"What are you doing here?"

"I'm on my way back to school." He was so pleased to see me! I moved into his smelly leather arms.

"Give me you number! I'll visit you next weekend."

I'd pined for him three years ago. Now he wouldn't let go of me: my first experience of reversal. So sweet!

"Where would you stay if you visited?"

"Your room." Dave kissed my mouth.

My father arrived; he looked confused.

"Go away," I thought I heard him say.

Dave shook my father's hand. Unlike me, my father did not dress for the day's potential glamour. His beige trench coat half matched his sturdy brown shoes, and his hard-backed briefcase seemed filled with bricks. Behind his glasses, his blue eyes asked silently *why am I here?*

The three of us sat in a line at the counter. I put a hand to my hair. I crossed and uncrossed my legs.

Dave pulled a salami sandwich from the pocket of his coat and began to eat it, almost offering bites, and then thinking better of it.

I sat for what felt like forever while gazing at the concourse, lunch and conversation forgotten. I peered sideways at my father—he looked like an intelligent animal too stunned to reach an arm through the bars, and open the unlocked cage.

Dave gulped his last crust. "I'll walk you to your train."

"Bye, Dad." I kissed his cheek, eager to resume my life apart, and left on Dave's arm. I felt it at my back: my father was forlorn.

On the train to Lawnhurst, Lisa sat surrounded by the Christmas gifts she'd purchased in a secondhand shop on Ninth Avenue: board books for baby Annabelle, Parcheesi for Aleksandar, patterned scarf for her mother, earrings for Therese. Therese would return the earrings by Valentine's Day, confessing, "she never wore them, and didn't want to waste their beauty." The chunky red plastic would accentuate the stiff minimalist dresses Lisa favored because they made her look weirder and more bohemian than she actually was. For her father, who tended to forget Modernists included women, the memoir *HERmione* by the poet H.D.

Lisa read the memoir while the train hurtled east. H.D. wrote she was "a disappointment to her father, an odd duckling to her mother, an importunate over-grown, unincarnated entity that had no place here." H.D. had written those lines in 1927. Over eighty years later, during feminism's "third wave," Lisa could relate. Yet she must pull herself together to marry Therese and Jude. She would simply act like a real officiant.

The station in Lawnhurst was not far from her parents' house. She went around back. The landing between the stairs to the basement and the kitchen was a good place to leave her boots; she felt a blister rising on her heel.

"I decided to do the food myself." Her mother Alice stood in the kitchen contemplating the table. Plastic bags of sliced rye bread, platters of bright green and red sliced peppers, steamed white cauliflower, rolls of meat and cheese. Shallow dishes filled with Dijon and whole grain mustard, empty little dishes waiting for dollops of mayonnaise. "What possessed me to do deli? It's a wedding, not a football game. I should have made roast chicken and orzo and goat cheese." Alice's interpretation of Mother of the Bride (marriage number two) was a leopard-spotted, silk, gathered-into-a-flattering-knot-at-the-waist, knee-length dress.

She was Lisa's original and best character—a flamboyant woman with outsized emotions, irrational desires, small secret hurts. This old-fashioned play complete with (hopeful, ridiculous) stage directions (directors made the actors do whatever the director fucking wanted the actors to do) was called *Coming Home*.

ALICE (*opening her arms*): You're a sight for sore eyes.
LISA (*enduring the embrace*): I'm sorry I've been so out of touch.
ALICE (*pushing her away*): Out of touch? Not calling or writing for nine months? You should be more than sorry! You should be ashamed of yourself! What's wrong with you? You've behaved so childishly! I'm so angry at you, I almost don't want to see you!
LISA (*holding out a hand*): But you do.

ALICE (*softening, taking her hand, hardening, squeezing it*): Are you sober?
LISA: Why is that always first? (*aside*) No one knows I'm grieving for Mark, no one can understand except Therese, and she'll never acknowledge it—she'd rather keep the tragedy all to herself.
ALICE (*affronted*): Being sober is first because it's most important. When I ask if you're sober I mean, are you really here? Are you thinking clearly?
LISA: I'm thinking more clearly now than ever.
ALICE: Good! Think about this then: how would you feel if I disappeared?
THERESE (*entering the kitchen wearing an off-the-shoulder, off-white lace dress; her feet bare, her polished toes hot pink*): If you disappeared, Ma? Are you kidding? She'd love it! We both would!
LISA (*warning*): Be nice, Therese.
ALICE: Yes, no brutality on your wedding day, dear. It's a tradition that must be observed, like wearing blue. Where's Aleksandar?
THERESE: With Dad. (*turning to Lisa*) So glad you could make it. Thanks for being our minister! Was it hard to get ordained?
LISA: Extremely hard. At the end of the Universal Life Church application it said, "if you do not get your confirmation email within 10 mins please check your junk/ spam filter."
THERESE: How many mins did it take?
LISA: About two.
ALICE: I'm going to find my shoes. (*muttering audibly under her breath as she exits*) These girls have made me insane.
THERESE: Mom wants everyone to stick with their parts

so she can keep playing hers; the big cheese. She needs Dad to act like however she thinks a "husband" should act so she can go on being his "wife." And if we don't play our parts as dutiful daughters, how can she be our "mother"?
LISA: When exactly have we ever been dutiful? Where's Dad?
THERESE: Where do you think? Hiding out.
LISA: And Jude?
THERESE: On his way, I hope. He's not responding to my calls or texts.
LISA: Are you worried?
THERESE: About Jude? No. Yes. No. I would be if he wasn't with Kevin.
LISA: He's a rock?
THERESE: He's dependable, which is more than I can say about you.
LISA: You're pissed because I've been AWOL, but I'm here now. I'm marrying you!
PAUL (*from off stage*): Is that who I think it is? Aleksandar! Come see your Aunt Lisa! (*He enters the kitchen holding Aleksandar with one arm, and hugs Lisa with the other.*)

Therese reached for Aleksandar, took him in her arms. Lisa watched her sister's face soften as Aleksandar rested his head on her shoulder. He popped his thumb into his mouth, and Therese gently brushed it out.

"You can meet Annabelle later. She's upstairs taking a nap. Your little hiatus away from the family is now officially over, Lisa," Therese said icily before leaving the kitchen.

As he grew older and more aware, would Therese be able to maintain her split personality? Maybe all parents hid their true selves from their kids.

"Dad," said Lisa. "I've missed you."

"Sweetheart," said her father, stepping back to look at her. He was still holding onto her arm. "I've missed you too. How was Vermont? Did you enjoy your residency at the arts center?" His blue oxford shirt matched his watery eyes. "Did you do some good writing?"

The talky intimacy she'd craved in college had never developed between them, but he was always kind.

"I did some writing."

"I'm sure it's good. Want to help me set up the tree?" Lisa followed her father into the living room.

Ancient ornaments, still in their crumbling boxes, were strewn across the cushions of the couch. The tree lay on the floor, the red and green metal tree stand in the corner, the large screws that would hold the tree in place turned just enough so they wouldn't fall out.

"Help me lift the tree, and we'll set it in the stand. I'll hold it while you get down beneath and tighten the screws. Remember to lift with your legs, not your back," said her father, and as she lifted, she remembered when he was stronger.

"Does it look straight?" she asked from under the tree, where the scent of pine was strong.

"Straight enough."

Lisa turned the screws until they gouged into the wood. "It needs water," she said, standing. Her father removed a needle stuck in her hair. "I'll get it."

On the kitchen counter were lemons, limes, tonic, soda, bottles of gin, vodka, and Scotch. Her bag sat on a chair tucked beneath the table. She wanted a sip from her flask, but if her father walked in, he'd think she was sneaking a drink. How had he maintained moderation all these years?

He behaved like a sailor entitled to two draughts per day, no more no less. (Not rum—vodka tonic.) Did he drink in secret? She did not think so. Were the two drinks always enough? How could they possibly be? So how did he accept, rather than resist or protest, when they weren't?

"What's your new play about?" asked her father when she had crawled back under the tree to tip the glass of water into the stand.

"Not sure yet honestly."

"Put these near the top," said her father when she stood up. He handed her a box of heavy silver ornaments shaped like candy canes and stockings. The center of each featured a photograph of her and Therese as cuddly toddlers. These photos held them spellbound when teenagers. How perfect they'd been when unconscious of their imperfection.

"Well, I can't wait to see your new play," said her father, taking the empty box, and handing over another filled with painted bells. "I love your plays."

Some people never seemed to internalize their shadow. Lisa thought of her friend Joy. Joy's artistic gifts were like the clear spring bubbling up from an unspoiled depth, running a course preordained by the universe. No one had ever built a belching factory on Joy's banks, or tried to dam her waters. Joy was intact. Until she'd met Joy, Lisa thought art always had to come, as it did from her, from brokenness.

"Lisa, the flowers are here," her mother called from upstairs. "Will you run outside and get them?"

"Yes," she called back.

At the back door, she shoved her feet into the boots again and walked around front without her coat, the blister on her heel rubbing with each step. It wasn't quite as cold on Long Island as it had been in Vermont, and it never got as dark. The sky here had a hazy imprecise quality—simultaneously close and far away—that Lisa associated with her father.

A wood-paneled station wagon was parked at the curb. It had been literally decades since Lisa had seen Kevin's Aunt Helen and his mother. Aunt Helen sat behind the wheel. Kevin's mother, in the passenger seat, rolled down the window, and stuck out her head.

"Oh my goodness, you look just like Therese!"

The recognition came to Lisa in a flash: the blurry gaze trying hard and failing to focus. Kevin's mother locked eyes with Lisa; Lisa could tell the recognition mutual.

I'm sober six months, Lisa wanted to say, but didn't.

"You're a dear for coming out to get the flowers. Helen hurt her ankle and it's still healing." Kevin's mother's Irish accent was still strong, her fragile eyes full of hope.

Lisa crouched next to the car to say hello, and Aunt Helen leaned forward to be seen. "Hello there," said Aunt Helen. "The flowers are on the back seat."

Lisa opened the car's back door.

"Holidays are tricky," cautioned Aunt Helen. "You don't want the flowers to look too Christmas-y, and you don't want them to clash with the other decorations."

Lisa crouched to slide her arm beneath the shallow cardboard box on which the flowers for the wedding all sat: white rose boutonnieres for the men, a white rose corsage for Alice, a mass of white hyacinth, jasmine and thick glossy greenery for the table, and two delicate white bouquets, one larger than the other, for the bride and maid of honor.

"Wow," said Lisa. "What a wonderful scent."

"Orange blossom," said Aunt Helen. "Shut your eyes and you're in Florida."

"I'm trying to sweeten your sour sister." Kevin's mother

laughed, coughed, lit a cigarette, the acrid smell of the match extinguishing the smell of flowers. "You haven't married, have you? My son is single too."

"Mind your business!" said Aunt Helen.

"Lisa," said Kevin's mother, "when it's time for you let me know, and I'll make you the perfect bouquet, the palest pink peonies, stock, a little freesia."

"Ignore her," recommended Aunt Helen.

"Thank you for the flowers," said Lisa, lifting them out of the car. She slammed the door just as she realized she should ask if they knew the whereabouts of Kevin and Jude.

Aunt Helen pulled away from the curb. Kevin's mother rolled up her window, leaving a crack for the smoke.

Running up and down the stairs getting Therese a glass of orange juice, finding the star for the top of the tree in the basement, looking in the attic for a shawl her mother knew was there in the navy garment bag though it wasn't, kept Lisa from worrying too much about officiating. She had written out her script, but Therese was a diva. There would be no way to follow it.

"Lisa, will you get the door?" yelled Alice from the bathroom when the bell rang.

"Jude is here, yes?" was the first thing Jude's mother Clara said when Lisa opened the door. She looked crushed when informed he wasn't.

"He'll be here, Mom. Jude is always late." Jude's sister Joanna stepped into the house behind her mother. "He likes to keep us guessing." Joanna was Therese's best friend, but had always been her opposite.

If Therese was borderline *Desperate Housewives*, Joanna was Pretty Mom: warm-toned clothes, heavy wedding ring, blow-dried hair. Her family entered the house behind her, her husband Sam and preteen kids, Teddy and Bee. Sam was still smiling, handsome, gentle. God, Joanna was lucky.

Lisa took everyone's coats and hung them in the closet, listening while Clara, Joanna, and Sam went into the living room and remarked on the beauty of the tree just as Alice came downstairs and accepted their compliments. Lisa returned to the living room to see her father offering Teddy and Bee a dish of red and green M & M's. The siblings' oily skin and hair glistened, radiating youth. Only the smattering of pimples on each of their chins marred the illusion of Roman god and goddess.

"It's probably Jude," said Lisa when the doorbell rang again. "I'll get it." She opened the door to find Mark's father, Adam.

Lisa opened her mouth and failed to close it, failed to find words—she had forgotten Adam looked so much like Mark, tall and thin and grief-stricken like Mark had so often been. Mark's darkness had somehow generated warmth. It was a known fact: everyone felt good around Mark, though Mark himself was needy, a bottomless pit.

Adam's darkness derived from masculine confidence. Because she could think of nothing to say, Lisa flung open her arms. The last time she had seen Mark's dad had been years ago, at Therese and Mark's wedding. Hugging Adam, she felt a dagger of desire; her body thought Adam was Mark. She let him go.

"Come on in." Lisa moved aside to let Adam pass, and thought of Hamlet's father, the ghost, muttering his lines: *Do not forget. This visitation / Is but to whet thy almost blunted purpose…* Adam was here to remind them his son was dead, to implore them not to forget Mark.

Back in the living room, Alice too-warmly greeted Adam, who ignored the tree. He walked toward Paul to shake hands.

"How the hell are you?"

"Happy Holidays," said Paul.

Lisa looked at her watch. The wedding was due to start, but still no groom. She imagined Therese upstairs, pacing.

"Pop Pop!" Aleksandar ran down the stairs and across the living room to Adam, who crouched to scoop him up. Aleksandar had the power to transform. A smile stretched Adam's face.

"Someone else is here," said Teddy, pointing out the window. "Two guys." Teddy reminded Lisa of the boy from her play, but his sister did too. They were at an androgynous age; everything for them was still a possibility.

"That's Jude and his best man, Kevin," said Alice.

I'd like a drink, thought Lisa. She went into the kitchen for her bag, her flask.

"The rings," she said out loud to no one in particular, and took the bag upstairs.

Therese was lying flat on her back on one of the old twin beds in the room they'd shared as kids. She put a finger to her lips. Annabelle was asleep in a porter crib between the beds.

"She's beautiful," Lisa whispered, before stretching out on the matching twin, though downstairs the doorbell rang, and everyone started talking and laughing more loudly. "Jude and Kevin are here."

"I know," whispered Therese. "Why do you think I can't hear? Do you think I should marry Jude?"

"Are those real questions?" asked Lisa.

"No," said Therese, sitting up. Her post-partum physicality was luscious, her rounded shoulders, her cleavage, her long curly hair. And in the lace dress—ugh. Lisa stopped looking, reached for her bag, pulled out her flask.

"No," said Therese. "Not today sweetheart, at least not right now."

"It's water," said Lisa. "Magic water that's almost gone." She put the flask to her lips.

"Bullshit," hissed Therese, grabbing her arm. "Give it to me; I'm the bride."

Lisa took a swallow and handed the flask to Therese. "You're getting the very last drop. You have no idea how generous I'm being."

Therese tipped back the flask. "It really is water!" she said. "You gave me a heart attack. I still don't know why I asked you to officiate. You don't deserve the honor. Mom's right. We should have put you in the stocks. You abandoned us."

"Do you have the rings?" asked Lisa. "You have them, right? Are you ready to tie the knot?"

"Tie the knot *again*, you mean?" asked Therese. "Because I definitely still feel married to Mark."

"Yeah," said Lisa. "I do too."

"What did you just say?" asked Therese.

"Therese!" a male voice called up the stairs.

"Kevin!" Therese called back. "Saved by Kevin," she muttered.

"Are you ladies ready?" Kevin stuck his head through the doorway, freshly shaved, and smelling deeply of weed.

"Is Jude stoned too?" asked Lisa.

"Of course not." Kevin's smile was as shy as his voice boisterous. "How you doing Lisa? I haven't seen you in what, a million years?"

"She's sober dude," said Therese, getting up from the bed to smooth her dress over her curves. Kevin whistled, but Lisa sensed it was out of duty and habit, and Therese's expectation of admiration. Or maybe he was whistling to endorse Lisa's sobriety. Now he was kneeling at the side of the crib, gazing at Annabelle.

"Here are the rings." Therese handed the tiny black box to Kevin. "I decided to leave Aleksandar out of the ceremony. He'll want to cuddle with Adam, his Pop Pop, his favorite," she said stoically, and held her left hand toward Lisa. "Take the ring," she said. "You have to pull, or it won't come. Wear it for me, will you?"

"Mark's ring?"

Therese nodded.

Lisa tugged the warm band of gold from Therese's finger and pushed it onto her own, expecting it to be loose, or too tight.

"How does it fit?" asked Kevin as he led the way down the stairs.

"Perfectly." Lisa knew she sounded pleased.

"Kev," said Therese. "You know Lisa is single?"

It was time to begin the ceremony. Lisa adjusted her A-line dress to hang straight from her shoulders. The velvet flats she'd slipped into were so soft her blister almost didn't hurt. Her MAC lipstick made her mouth feel protected and important. Everyone circled in the living room. They were all looking at her. She held out her hands in a gesture of welcome, smiling warmly at wily Jude, who'd gained a surprising amount of weight, but still looked good in his dark suit.

Lisa raised her eyebrows: Are you really ready to marry my sister? Jude nodded yes.

LISA: Remember how alive you felt when you were young, how fast you moved, how you laughed so easily, and frequently cried? How exceedingly difficult, no, how impossible it was until you were older and slower, for you to understand, even a little, what had happened to you when you were young? When you were finally able to gather the bits and pieces, adding them to form what you believe to be a cohesive whole? You still look back and feel raw and embarrassed, but you find yourself seeing your mother or father or brother or sister's point of view, find yourself looking at their images or even your own with tenderness, and in so doing see some detail, a chin, or collarbone, or hand, or hip, for which you feel new sympathy.

THE CURTAIN FALLS

Acknowledgments

Many thanks to the editors who published earlier versions of these stories: Carolyn Kuebler, editor of *The New England Review*, Dan DeWeese, editor of *Propeller*, Peter Stitt, editor of the *Gettysburg Review*, Sid Miller and Adam O'Connor Rodriguez, editors of the *Burnside Review*, and Roelof Bakker, photographer and editor of the book *Still: Short Stories Inspired by Photos of Vacated Spaces*.

Thank you to George Saunders for feedback on "The Loop Trail," and thank you to the many writers who have helped make these stories stronger: Veer Frost, Dawna Kemper, Joan Dempsey, Christa Mastroangelo, Evan P. Schneider, Natalie Serber, Laura Moulton, and Lee Montgomery.

For camaraderie, support, and inspiration, thank you to writers Alex Behr, Amanda Gersh, Apricot Irving, and Susan Moore.

Thank you avid readers Judith Evans, Rachel Greben, Dina Levy, and Jennifer Rechner for your insightful feedback as well as for your time and care with my work.

Thank you Betsy Amster, for believing in these characters and helping to bring them to life and print. Thank you Heather Brown, for getting the word out!

Dan DeWeese, editor and friend, thank you for believing in my work.

Elyssa, Jen, Heather, Beth, Kim, Amy, Ellen, Barbara, and Christy, thank you for the gift of your friendship.

Thank you to my loving, supportive, and creative family, Mom and Dad, Mike, Jennifer, Jessica, Matthew, Christopher, Jeannie, my mother-in-law Betty, my brothers and sisters-in-law, and all my nieces and nephews.

Dan and Ollie, thank you for inspiring, challenging, and loving me. It's a gift and a joy to be your mom.

Barry, thank you for your love and trust and confidence—in me, in yourself, in us.

About the Author

Mary Rechner is the author of *Nine Simple Patterns for Complicated Women*, named to the long list for the Frank O'Connor International Short Story Award, and the novella *The Opposite of Wow*, published in the *Hong Kong Review*. Her fiction has appeared in publications such as *New Letters*, *Harvard Review*, *Gettysburg Review*, *New England Review*, *Kenyon Review*, and *Washington Square*. Her criticism and essays have appeared in *Litro*, *The Believer*, *Oregon Humanities*, and the *Oregonian*. A recipient of fellowships from Literary Arts and the Regional Arts and Culture Council, as well as residencies from Caldera and the Vermont Studio Center, Rechner taught fiction writing at Portland State University and the University of Portland and now teaches media arts to high school students.

Printed in the USA
CPSIA information can be obtained
at www.ICGtesting.com
JSHW021523020923
47379JS00003B/15